THE LAST PHOTOGRAPH

STEPHEN BRANSFORD

THOMAS NELSON PUBLISHERS
Nashville • Atlanta • London • Vancouver

Published in Nashville, Tennessee, by Thomas Nelson, Inc., Publishers, and distributed in Canada by Word Communications, Ltd., Richmond, British Columbia.

Scripture quotations are from the NEW KING JAMES VERSION of the Bible, Copyright © 1979, 1980, 1982, Thomas Nelson, Inc., Publishers.

Library of Congress Cataloging-in-Publication Data

Bransford, Stephen, 1949–
    The last photograph : a story of brothers / Stephen Bransford.
       p. cm.
    "A Jan Dennis book."
    ISBN 0-7852-8011-1
    1. Fathers and sons—United States—Fiction. 2. Brothers—United States—Fiction. I. Title.
PS3552.R326L37 1995
813'.54—dc20   95-45836
                                                  CIP

Printed in the United States of America

1 2 3 4 5 6 — 00 99 98 97 96 95

TABLE OF CONTENTS

For Tara, Josh, Tyler, and Colter

After the fire a still small voice

1 Kings 19:12

THE PORTRAIT

A line of eight horsemen and six loaded pack mules ambled from a band of evergreens high above Idaho's Selway River. The October sun burned low in the sky, lengthening the shadows and deepening the colors of the season. Horses wheezed, mules grunted, and shod hooves clicked on stone. As the riders approached the breaks of the gorge, a damp breeze pressed suddenly against their faces like an eager spirit released from the river's deep crevasse. They shivered, tugging at kerchiefs, coats, hats, and mufflers, resisting the phantom wind.

From my place near the back of the wilderness caravan, I could see Gordon, our bearded outfitter, leading the way, towing three pack animals. Above the broad shoulders of his faded denim jacket, a light tan Stetson turned persistently left and right as his eyes swept the terrain ahead, absorbing details of pasture, game, trail, and weather. My backside view of his soiled hat brim had not varied for the past seven hours. He was not only our guide, he was my older brother, and where he led, as usual, I followed.

Behind Gordon rode Tim, our younger brother, wearing a Mongolian fur hat. Fresh from a foreign embassy assignment, he had imported an international flair into this family adventure.

Dad followed next, hunched in a green slicker and crowned with a baseball cap of plaid wool. His coarse three-day beard underscored his nickname, "Griz." We sometimes called him "Sourdough Griz," especially when he prepared his fermented pancakes. At other times he received the full title, "The Reverend Sourdough Griz," because first and foremost, he was a preacher.

Behind Griz rode his younger brother Dick, a polished New Mexico horseman. He was followed by my brother-in-law Jerry and Griz's youngest brother, Bob. I rode next to last in line, followed by Cheryl, Gordon's wife. She led three more pack mules at the rear of our train.

The distant roar of white water sighed in our ears as Gordon led us onto a barren hogback ridge. We could see our trail winding along its exposed spine for another quarter-mile. Ahead in the fading light appeared the balding half-dome of Otter Butte. Its timbered shoulder revealed the sapling poles and white canvas walls of a wilderness campsite: our home for the next ten days. I began to dream of hot chocolate, good grub, and a warm sleeping bag.

Riding with gloved hands folded beneath the armpits of a mackinaw, I leaned back in the saddle and stared vacantly until recognition hit me. At the far end of the ridge, a rock outcropping beckoned, offering the kind of position that would let me photograph the entire pack train as it approached. I had looked for this all day.

Forgetting the weariness and cold, I reached behind the saddle for a Nikon-EM nestled in the pack. I had shot dozens of pictures from the saddle already. Without looking now, I could find the camera by feel. Swinging it around, I hesitated; it held black-and-white film. The fall colors blazed around us. I could reload with Kodachrome to capture their glory, but precious seconds would be lost. If I wanted the picture at all, even in black and white, I would have to move fast.

Spurring my horse, I overtook Uncle Bob riding ahead, handing him my reins. "Never mind me, Bob. Keep moving."

With that, I swung a leg over the saddle and jumped free. A surprising pain shot across the arches of my feet as they hit the ground. Hours of balancing in the stirrups had shut off normal circulation. Stumbling awkwardly, I began to hurry ahead.

"Got a horsefly in his pants," quipped Tim as I ran past his mount.

"What's that recruit up to now?" Griz chuckled. I could almost visualize his plaid hat wagging at my antics.

"I've seen this before," kidded Gordon, turning sideways in the saddle to watch my unexplained approach. "Steve's gone 'Rocky Mountain high.' Yup. Flatlanders get crazy up here in this rarified air."

As if on cue, my boots slipped on a mound of bunch

grass and spilled me face forward. I hit the sidehill, using my elbows to protect the camera's zoom lens. The pack animals snorted and shied, showing the whites of their eyes as I rolled painfully to my feet below the trail. As I checked my bruises and reconsidered the effort, the other riders reined in to control their horses.

"Never seen anyone work that hard for a picture," Dick commented.

Neither had I, and especially not me, but I had no time to explain. I could see the rock outcropping another three hundred yards ahead, an exhausting run for me. Yet I could project the scene from there—the "magic hour" had arrived; fading daylight would surround each rider with a halo of backlight. *Too good to pass up*, I thought, so I took off running again. Gordon's spurs jingled softly as I passed him. Behind me, the pack train resumed its plodding motion.

Oxygen-thin air seared my lungs and worked my leg muscles like a wrangler's knot. But I knew better than to ask my brother to stop the pack train, just to allow me to get into position. Even if he had understood my intentions perfectly, the outfitter-horseman would not have delayed his animals' rendezvous with oats and hay, which lay another twenty minutes ahead in camp. Knowing this, I felt that I had to press on.

As I ran, I was reminded that much more than a photo opportunity drove my churning legs. How could I explain to the others that I was responding to an inner voice? If they knew the whole truth, they might dismiss me as being crazy.

I had heard the voice two months before, at home in North Carolina while standing on my backyard patio near a storage shed. Summer had begun to wane. With each breath of breeze, the surrounding elms and maples whispered of fall's approach. As I sorted gear for the upcoming hunt, I thought back to my brother's invitation: At our 1979 family reunion in Seattle, he had offered all the men of our extended family, free of charge, a ten-day Idaho elk hunting expedition with his Selway-Bitterroot outfit. He would serve as our guide. We had eagerly signed up and had been making plans ever since.

I now broke out hunting equipment and made a checklist to see that nothing essential had been left out. I had shaken out a sleeping bag, stuffed it in a rucksack, tossed in some newly purchased insulated boots, a hunting knife, a bone saw, a compass, a topographical map of the Selway-Bitterroot Wilderness, a pair of Woolrich overpants, toiletries, chocolate bars, raisins, a copy of the book *Writing for the Outdoor Market*—who knows, I thought, I might write off some expenses with a magazine deal—a mackinaw, two pairs of duofold underwear, a Nikon camera, extra boxes of 180-grain Silvertip cartridges, and the old model 721 Remington .30-06 calibre rifle with its open peep sight.

I paused in my packing to remove the weapon from its storage case, holding it again for the first time in thirteen years. Tracing its graceful walnut stock, I could see that the finish bore scars from sun, rain, snow and from an occasional tumble in rough terrain. These were the scars of my growing years. Having not seen the gun for so long, my thoughts rushed back to those younger days. The gun had been a present from Griz on my twelfth birthday.

Griz and the gun. Everything I felt about that rifle was somehow interwoven with my feelings about him. As memories often do, my first thought recalled the best of times. I remembered with pride his supreme compliment; "Old Dead Eye," he had shouted, slapping me on the back enthusiastically for a superior display of marksmanship. I also remembered that the compliment had been special because it had been so painfully won. When I had first attempted to shoot, Griz had called me a "raw recruit" for incompetence. In his vernacular, I "couldn't hit the broad side of a barn" back then. I burned again, recalling those words.

At times, I mused, Dad could fit his grizzly nickname well. He exhibited the fathering sensibilities of the king of bears. Yet he added to that brute toughness the surprising spirituality of a prophet, which made him a complex character, indeed. To properly appreciate Griz, one had to understand his unique combination of physical presence and piety. Truly, if I had met John the Baptist in camel's hair, I would have met his equal.

Prior to my birth in 1949—another in the postwar baby boom—Griz had lived the hard-working, drinking, brawling life of a lumberjack. Among the antiunionist elite "jippo" loggers of Oregon—those paid by the board foot rather than by the hour—he had earned the coveted title "timberbeast." Then unexpectedly Griz had "met the Lord." His remarkable turnabout happened in a gospel tent, set up on a street corner in our little town. After "going forward" and "giving his life to the Lord," Griz promptly gave up his timberbeast title, announcing a "call to preach."

Some of the locals suggested that he had merely been confused by the smell of sawdust on the floor. They doubted that he had truly got religion. In that respect, his former tavernmates and fellow loggers would not let the conversion pass untested. They tested and he passed, but decidedly not by turning the other cheek. Rather, he invented his own brand of witness, declaring his newfound faith boldly and challenging anyone who belittled it to show themselves the better man. This approach bore fruit in the Oregon of 1949. Before long, several of Oregon's toughest lumberjacks became church-going deacons under Grizzly's two-fisted influence.

For the next five years he took Bible and theology courses under the tutelage of a local pastor, finally becoming a fully licensed preacher. His lumberjacking began to fade, but never the hunting and fishing. He remained an unusual combination of outdoorsman-preacher in the communities he served. His rough-cut mode appealed to the kind of man who lived and worked in the Great Northwest more than the seminary-softened style of other ministers, which mostly pleased females.

Pondering these things anew on my Carolina patio, my thoughts turned from Griz to the gun in my hands. Standing before that pile of hunting gear, I worked the rifle's bolt, opening the breach. The familiar smell of Hoppe's cleaning solvent and burnt powder triggered a host of new memories.

I recalled shooting the gun for the first time on my twelfth birthday. Griz had loaded Gordon and me into his yellow Willys "four-banger" jeep and had driven us to an eastern Oregon basalt mesa, explaining the virtues of my military peep sight as we went. He seemed proud that he had found what he considered to be the perfect shooting system for me, his second son, now becoming a young man.

"It gives a wider field of vision," he explained. "You learn to aim more by feel than logic. All it takes is some shooting and you'll be able to pick a tick off a buck's rack at a hundred yards."

He seemed quite sure of this, but I had no idea what he meant.

"You can keep your military peepers," my brother Gordon scoffed.

My older brother, who was fourteen and a half at the time, often surprised me with comments like these. First of all, it mystified me that he always seemed to know what Griz was talking about. Even more remarkably, he had expressed a contrary opinion. I seldom had an opinion, and never one that opposed Dad. If I did, I had the good sense to keep it to myself.

"I'll take my buckhorn sights over that peep any day," Gordon went on, brandishing his own Enfield .30-06. "When I put my bead on an animal I want to know exactly where my bullet's going. No guesswork."

"Well, you're right," Griz responded. "The buckhorn is the right system for you, son."

The comment amazed me. Gordon had not only opposed Griz, he had been declared right. If I had tried it, I would have earned a good hard look of scorn at the very least.

"Some people just shoot better with that buckhorn," Griz concluded. "A guy can't argue with a good shot."

Well, there it was: "a good shot." That description removed me from the conversation entirely. At the age of twelve, I had yet to shoot a big game rifle, and I had a feeling that beginner's luck was not about to bless me simply because it was my birthday.

At the mesa Gordon and Griz blasted several dime-size holes through the center of a tin can. Then, Griz turned proudly and handed the smoking cannon to me. As I stared, trembling, I briefly recalled my wish for a twelve-stringed mandolin. A black evangelist had played one at church, and every note from his fingertips had touched some deep emotional chord in my heart. For a moment, I thought that if a boy approaching his twelfth birthday asks his father-with-the-sensitivities-of-a-grizzly-bear for a musical instrument—he might just get a big game rifle, instead. It was one of those opinions I kept to myself.

Trying to look grateful, I pried my hands from over my ears to receive my birthday present. Both Griz and Gordon scowled. In those days we believed that only girls and sissies plugged their ears at the sound of rifle fire. I had definitely cast myself with the wrong crowd here. The violent explosion of their shooting, even though it had been muffled beneath my sweaty palms, had convinced me that the weapons were not for killing deer but for wiping out the entire species in a single blast. Had I been allowed to choose right then and there, I would have accepted my birthday present and waited years to initiate it. But that would have disappointed Griz, something akin to disappointing God in my mind.

With growing dread I slid my too-thin fingers around the rifle's stock. Stretching my arms to their limit, I pointed and squinted through the military peep, attempting to find the tin can. Immediately I wondered how anyone could hit anything with it. The gold bead on the end of the barrel moved like a firefly through the rear sighting circle. There seemed to be altogether too much room for error in the system. How could Griz say it was right for me? Try as I would, my skinny arms could not hold the gun steady, so, using my best judgment, I closed both eyes and pulled the trigger just to get it over with. *Thunder! Lightning!* I leaped backward like a sapling hit by a bulldozer.

They laughed. "Not bad for a start," Griz said, "but I can see we've got a few more lessons to learn here. You can't hit the broad side of a barn shooting with your eyes closed."

I could hardly wait to go through this punishment again. What a birthday! My ears rang, the bone joints in my skull throbbed, and my right shoulder felt like it had been kicked by an angry mule.

Gordon stopped laughing long enough to inform me that while I had failed to hit the broad side of a barn, I *had* managed to "vaporize a fist-sized chunk of Oregon, sending it into the primordial void from whence it came." In our family, vivid verbal descriptions were prized—perhaps because our father, though rough-hewn, preached that way. Gordon tended to use his own secular forms of hyperbole with me, even to describe busting a dirt clod with a big game bullet.

Meanwhile, the tin can sat there mocking me. As a son of Griz, I had hoped to inherit marksmanship, but no chance. Such skill had to be earned through trial and error. Many trips to the mesa would be required before I could shoot without sissy earplugs, or handle the shoulder-bruising kick of a 180-grain Silvertip breaching the muzzle with 2,910 foot-pounds of energy. Compared to Gordon's early shooting record, mine seemed an unduly long struggle.

Finally, it happened. On that long road from boyhood to *griz*hood, from wanting a mandolin to wanting to put meat on the table, time itself took me through a desensitization process. Two years later, dime-size holes began to appear in a few tin cans placed before me at one hundred yards. If I might say so, I eventually became a darn good shot.

Griz, in his grizzly wisdom, turned out to be exactly right about the open peep sight. Once I overcame fear of the gun, it fit my personality like a glove. I aimed better by feel than by logic. My eye would naturally center the sight for me, and I eventually competed well with Gordon, knocking down some difficult game. On one occasion, a running deer had gone down, heart-shot at more than three hundred yards.

In my Carolina yard, I lifted the rifle again and squinted through the peep at a spot on the patio floor, recalling the last time I had fired the gun. A spike bull elk had gone down with a single bullet to the heart during my senior year in high school—no doubt my best moment as a hunter. By then, I had added logic to my intuitive shooting style.

It had been a difficult shot through brush, aiming at a

forty-degree angle downhill. Having memorized the bullet's trajectory before the season, I had mentally calculated its path against the diminished pull of gravity. I had also learned from watching Gordon that the bull's apparent broadside position on the hillside below was an illusion. For all of that I compensated, aiming high, near the backbone just behind the shoulder blades. Closing one eye, I had steadily squeezed until the pressure released the lead from its brass cartridge, and in that split second before the recoil slammed my cheek and shoulder, I had seen the bull begin to fall.

Rushing down the steep hillside I arrived at about the same time as Griz. The animal lay as if asleep. His great heart had stopped instantly. It was time to start dressing his carcass for the meat locker.

"Old Dead Eye!" Griz had enthused, slapping me on the back powerfully enough to leave me coughing on the hillside. For all my growing efforts as a hunter, that had been his supreme compliment, hearty, unrestrained, and hard-earned in my view.

Reflecting on the skill of that shot, I mused, if only my older brother, Gordon, had seen it. But he had been serving in Vietnam during one of the bloodiest years of the war. He could not have related to anything so trivial as my taking a spike bull.

As I continued preparations for the upcoming Idaho hunt, I wondered if I could shoot that well again after thirteen years. Not without practice. I would probably have to start all over again at a local rifle range, flinching and closing my eyes like a raw recruit. But I made up my mind right then that I would pay the price of a black-and-blue shoulder, and do it.

My competitive feelings toward Gordon remained surprisingly strong in 1980. Even though the years had passed between us, I still wanted to beat him at the shooting game. Here I was, a grown man, determined to finish our boyhood contest.

Recalling how the rivalry started, I remembered that it had eventually grown pretty intense, like most of our differences. Above all, we valued a good clean kill. Most of our kills were head or neck shots. In more difficult circumstances we allowed for a heart shot. We considered it a great crime to miscalculate the location of the vital organs and cause an animal to suffer before death. To gut-shoot deserved the stocks. Neither did we forgive the ruining of table steaks and roasts by poorly placed bullets. Griz had taught us to respect the deer and elk we killed, and since our family depended on them for food, we competed mercilessly over matters of shooting skill.

At the height of those skillful years Gordon and I invented a mealtime ritual. We would celebrate our shooting statistics at the table as we passed the plates of tender venison around: *". . . head-shot, neck-shot, heart-shot . . . on a dead run at two hundred yards!"* By bragging about marksmanship, it was as if we wanted the other members of our family to eat with a feeling of great obligation, something akin to worship, toward one or the other of us, the mighty hunters of the family. Griz seemed supremely proud of the ritual. It was outdoor stuff, which pleased him like a bruin in a patch of wild huckleberries.

Between 1967 and 1980, a competitive gap remained between Gordon and me. I had lost my competitive foil when he had gone to Vietnam, which turned out to be the time I had become the better shot between us. Without him around to appreciate it—or more accurately, for me to rub his nose in it—the achievement had lost its kick. There remained some nose rubbing for me to do on this upcoming hunt.

Could I prove myself the mightiest hunter of the clan again? Would I pull off the best shot, the cleanest kill, and win Griz's and Gordon's highest praise? Would I resurrect "Old Dead Eye" and mount the largest trophy of the Idaho hunt?

That is when the voice broke in: *Give your brother his place!* The command scattered my self-absorbed thoughts like leaves.

How can I describe the voice? It was not audible, but as effective as if it *had* been. It formed words inside of me. Like using the open peep sight, each syllable jolted me with a palpable recoil, and without effort, hit a meaningful bullseye in my heart. I could immediately feel the importance of letting Gordon have his place, especially now that we had become men. Our whole lives had been defined by competition. The time had come for appreciation. However, appreciation would not come naturally to me where he was concerned.

Sobered, I slowly set my rifle against the storage shed wall. I began reasoning within myself: *Why do I carry on this childish duel with Gordon? It doesn't make sense anymore. I have moved on with my life. I have my own career, my special place in the family. Why keep clawing for recognition; trying to be the best, the biggest, the most?* For a moment all I could hear were the cicadas humming steadily in the trees and shrubs around the yard.

Say absolutely nothing of yourself on this trip, the inner voice broke in. *Instead, celebrate your brother's life.*

The message had taken on new urgency, and more than that, it had added a new difficulty factor. I would never ask such a thing of myself—to celebrate my brother's life while at the same time keeping absolutely silent about my own. Given our lifelong contentions, that seemed beyond reason. Maybe when I grew very old that kind of maturity would emerge from me, but not now. I could get a piece of my act together temporarily, but not all of it at once, and surely not in time for the hunt.

I began to argue with the voice for leniency: *It's just like nothing has changed between us since the days we passed the venison plate at the family table. I brag—we both brag. It's as natural as breathing.*

I recalled an exchange between us at the Seattle Christmas reunion. "We're thinking of buying the adjacent outfit next year," Gordon had said, proud of the expansion of his young business.

Reflexively I had interjected, "Did you hear that a motion picture company is buying an option on my screenplay?"

What did that comment have to do with anything? Nothing, except that it steered attention away from him, and toward me. The sour atmosphere my comment had created between us seemed obvious, but I could not recall having one thought beforehand that might have prevented it. The words had just popped out because I was always out to get one up on him. It was bound to happen again on the upcoming hunt.

But the inner voice had demanded that I stop all of that nonsense and celebrate my brother's life. I sighed hopelessly, stuffing my hands into my pockets, rocking back and forth in front of the growing pile of hunting equipment on the patio floor. To do as the voice suggested would require an unprecedented amount of willpower on my part.

"OK," I said to the inner voice, "let's say you've got a fine idea. But don't ask me to do the impossible. Let's just take a small step now. We can do more later. Besides, I've never been much good at sheer willpower. How can I do this thing at all? I mean *really* do it?"

My eyes swept absently across the hunting gear near my feet as I pondered the dilemma. The thought came to me that if I expected to break a lifetime habit, I might need some help, a crutch. Or better yet, a tool to redirect all of my bragging energies into obeying the command of the still small voice: *"Keep quiet and celebrate your brother."*

That is when my eyes fell across the answer: the new automatic Nikon-EM. It lay on a stack of long underwear, all black and glossy with promise, a precision-crafted professional's tool designed for the amateur like me. It suddenly hit me that the perfect crutch, the perfect tool for obeying the voice, would be that camera with its zoom lens.

From my limited experience, I had learned that cameras do not operate well in the hands of self-absorbed people. Especially not the single lens reflex camera. Even though mine was a new automatic model, it still required manual focusing and aperture selection. Photography would discipline me to project outward, concentrating on lens speed, shutter speed, film speed, aperture, light, and composition. And I would be forced to apply all this technical knowledge to others. Furthermore, after the hunt, there would be no better way to give my brother his place and celebrate his life than in an album of hunting memories presented to him and all our related families for the Christmas season to follow. If during the hunt I put myself completely into the camera, there would be little time or temptation to talk of myself. What better tool could I possibly find?

Picking up the camera, I felt an immediate exhilaration. It was as if I had stepped into a new dimension of possibilities. Rather than concentrating on shooting my gun, in preparation for the Idaho hunt I would visit a professional camera store, seeking the best advice I could find so that my efforts would produce an album of memorable pictures. Which is the whole reason why, two months later, I found myself running like a flatlander, pushing myself to get to the rock outcropping on the end of that Idaho ridge before the rest of the hunters.

I panted to a stop, climbing into place above the trail. As I looked backward, the pack string ambled along the land bridge two hundred yards behind, giving me time to catch my breath. I mentally called roll as I watched their progress; Gordon, Tim, Griz, Uncle Dick, Jerry, Uncle Bob, who now led my empty mount, and Cheryl.

I raised the zoom lens, focused wide and captured the group using a fast, 1/125-second shutter speed to compensate for my shaking hands and heavy breathing. Reframing, I fired twice more. Each time I tripped the shutter, I listened for that quiet inner impression—the voice. I wanted to hear it whisper, "*Well done,*" if for no other reason than I barely rated as an amateur photographer and needed reassurance. I wanted to hear, *"That's the picture you are supposed to take."*

I heard nothing. No sense of warmth or well doing. No inner message. So I lowered the camera and waited.

At the age of thirty-one, I had already been jolted by a few of life's surprises. As a result, I had gained a new respect for its mystery. I trusted my own abilities much less these days. I had learned that when I charged ahead without opening my eyes and ears to new possibilities, I often missed important details, even in something as ordinary as shooting a photograph.

As the riders wound their serpentine path toward me I noticed how tired and solemn they had grown. By contrast, they had been in high spirits at the Indian Hill base camp, dining on generous helpings of pancakes, eggs, bacon, and hash browns. Their elation had been fueled by the sight of a six-by-nine trophy elk taken on the hunt preceding ours. Expectations had soared at the prospects of taking more such bulls in the backwoods. But the energy of that high-spirited breakfast had deserted them. Their bodies, like mine, ached for arrival in the wilderness camp.

Next, I noticed the figure of my father. Not as ramrod straight in the saddle as he had been as a younger man, he seemed weighed by more than simple age and fatigue. Griz, the outdoorsman-preacher, oldest of three brothers, father to three sons, had passed on his love for the great outdoors to all of his boys. However, he had not been universally successful in sharing his love for God. Gordon, always independent, had grown bitter toward religion and the church, especially after his years of service in Vietnam. Though he and Griz showed similar personality traits—decisive, hard, absolutist—family reunions found them holding court at opposite ends of the household. The pain of this religious fracture throbbed beneath much of our family conversation.

As he often made clear, Griz tolerated no religious doubts. He knew what doubts were, too. Prior to his conversion in that 1949 tent meeting, he had been morally confused by his own hypocrisy. During the Second World War he had engaged in a reckless lifestyle that had undermined his better judgment. He had needed to be saved, and he knew it. He blamed no one else for his folly. In that regard, the life-changing beliefs he embraced on the sawdust trail had proven far from trivial. His consistent lifestyle since could be traced to that very event. Our family knew Griz not as one who had become religious but as one who had entered a personal relationship with God Almighty through a clear revelation of Truth—spelled with the largest capital "T" available. In our collective lifetimes we had never seen a hypocritical act from our dad, a distinction none of us seemed able to match.

By contrast, doubts and questions had constantly emerged in our growing minds. We were children who had not committed the sins of our father; our repentance could never seem quite as deep as his. His conversion had produced a quantum leap in terms of change; ours had been like crossing a street. Also, as we grew up, the moral certainty that had blessed the World War II generation began to abandon ours. Through the '50s and '60s we struggled to remain true to the faith in the shadow of the nuclear threat, the Cuban Missile Crisis, the assassinations of Kennedy and King, "situational ethics," Elvis, The Beatles, and the sudden availability of something called "the pill." An America that had once seemed predictable and sane, became crazy like a carnival ride. As we had listened to Dad's morally black-and-white sermons at church—even preaching against going to movies and watching TV—he began to sound out of step with the subtleties of our times, perhaps even uninformed. Helping his children maintain a solid faith in those days required more nurture than Griz could readily get his hands on. We grew apart. Yet we loved him and he loved us. That certainty held at the center of our confused lives.

Nothing meant more to Griz than the ultimate salvation of our souls. "I want to see all my kids in heaven," he would often repeat. So, most of us went to great lengths to reassure him, and ourselves, about our ultimate destination. All of us did, that is, except Gordon. He defied this unwritten rule of the family faith, living his life in rebellion against the things Griz remained careful to observe: Bible reading, prayer, church attendance, teetotalism, and clean language.

With all that in mind, I looked again at the stoop to my father's shoulders and knew that not only age pulled at his frame but sadness of the deepest sort. I raised the camera and fired again. This time I could feel a moment of truth pass onto the film. Frozen for time, I'd caught Gordon riding lead—young, hard, and proud—Griz following in the distance, stooped and labored. It would make a good private picture, I thought, since only I would understand it. But something more waited out there to be captured on film. Something about my brother. After all, the voice had directed me to celebrate his life on this hunt.

The pack train grew nearer to my position and loomed larger in the lens. Suddenly a new angle inspired me. If I moved to the left of the rock outcropping, I'd be able to shoot a portrait of Gordon as he broke the crest of the ridge alone. The new position would frame the tough mountain cowboy against the wilderness he knew and loved so well.

I leaped from the tallest rock outcropping and headed for a small pile of loose shale below, all the while keeping my eyes on the trail and the background that would appear behind the shot as I snapped it. The combination of foreground and background would be everything to this picture. To properly match them I would have to position the camera lens at just the right elevation. Too high, and I would lose the magic of the distant ridge. Too low, and I would produce an unreadable silhouette against the sky. I continued to watch the juxtaposition as I moved.

Finding what seemed to be the best angle, I dropped to one knee and lifted the Nikon. The composition of the scene Gordon would soon enter demanded a vertical format, I could see that right away. I turned the camera to match it. Dialing the aperture-controlled lens to a normal, sixtieth of a second shutter speed, I held my breath for steadiness.

A point of shale began to bite mercilessly into the bone of my knee. Glancing down, I quickly located a smoother rock nearby. Bracing myself against it, I waited again, filling with anticipation. This is it, I sensed, this is the picture. I prefocused, twisting the lens to sharpen the brush near the spot where he would appear. All was ready.

Suddenly he rode into view, filling the eyepiece from Stetson to chaps, a bearded, long-haired, outlaw of a man. Eyes narrowed, he fixed me from beneath his weathered hat brim. His right hand lightly held a braided horsehair rein while his left remained open in the loop of the lead line. Behind him the barren ridge stretched out, pierced along its way by the steeple-spired Engelmann spruce. He looked the part he played in life: a philosophical poet-cowboy and Vietnam vet, who loved to sit under the stars with a shot of Jack Daniels in his coffee, listening to coyotes howl, talking of Indian legend, archaeology, the origin of the species; and on rare occasions among family and friends, expounding his troubled understanding of God.

Click, went the shutter. "*Well done,*" whispered the inner voice, "*that is the picture you are supposed to take.*"

Gordon rode past on my right as I wound off the roll of film and wiped sweat from my forehead. "I got a picture of you, big brother," I managed to say, still trembling from running the length of the ridge.

I'll never forget the look he gave me. He paused. For a moment his eyes lost their narrowed mask and widened as if awakening from a half-sleep. The hard cowboy vanished and only my brother remained. He smiled unguardedly as if appreciating how I had pushed myself down that long ridge to secure his portrait. But the smile was for more than that. The meaning of the photograph had grown for both of us from another meeting we had shared three years ago, when we had talked into the night, discussing this time and place as a distant dream. Now the dream had come true, and I had captured it. He seemed to be remembering all of that as he paused, then shook his spurs and rode on.

A glow of satisfaction spread through me as Bob arrived with my horse. Mounting again, I wondered if I had perhaps conjured the instructions of the inner voice. Had I subconsciously engineered this experience? I dismissed the question. It didn't matter. I thought the moment ranked as a personal treasure. Why quibble with it?

But I had no way of knowing the full significance of what I had just done. A year later I would begin to understand, after a series of events made it clear that the voice had come from a providential source beyond my imagination. Only then did I begin to sort through the years with Gordon, collecting a mosaic of evidence that deepened my appreciation for our rare moment on the ridge. The incident soon became a marker, a milestone, reminding me of the wonderful things I would surely miss in life, if Divine Grace did not stoop to correct my human agendas.

RITES OF PASSAGE

Gordon and I seemed destined to rub each other the wrong way. He was born with spurs on, I was a natural tenderfoot. As we grew, he enjoyed physical labor; I ran from it. He feared nothing; I battled terrors and phobias. His energies burst in an outward direction while mine had remained moody and inward. He formed clubs and gangs with his buddies; I played games with imaginary friends. He always knew exactly what he wanted; I chronically wondered what life was all about. He played sports; I spent time in the library. He would dive head first into rivers; I would dip in a toe, turn blue, and seldom swim. He liked to wear dirty, worn-out clothes; I liked to dress up. He liked dogs, cows, pigs, horses—anything animal; I preferred things ethereal.

To my mind, the most enduring mystery about Gordon

was how he could take a belt-whipping from Griz and not shed a tear. This form of punishment, I recall most vividly, coming our way between the ages of five and ten. Unlike Gordon, I would cry for a half hour before Griz ever touched me.

Anticipating judgment's arrival in my bedroom, sometimes twenty minutes to an hour would pass before the cleansing lashes Griz had promised were actually applied to my backside. In the meantime, I twisted slowly in a wind of my own making, a wail issuing between my clenched jaws like the sound bursting from the lungs of a yearling calf during branding. Running in place added an interesting vibrato to the howl, as did pleading over and over, "No, no, no, please Daddy, no!" I would often end choking here, drawing a huge breath before starting all over again.

Gordon, who may or may not have been promised the same thrashing—it mattered not—would enter our shared bedroom, take one look at me, and break up laughing. "What's the matter with you? It's only a whipping, for heaven's sake."

I hated him.

My tears earned only Gordon's disgust. Boys were not to be sensitive in his book. "Crybaby," he called me. He swore he couldn't take me anywhere for fear that I would embarrass him in front of his friends.

He remained my tormenter for most of our years together, figuring that since I was a crybaby, he might as well amuse himself and give me something to cry about. In grammar school, he joined the football team and made me practice blocking him. I got banged around and—what else—I cried. He joined the wrestling team and would badger me into wrestling him on the living room carpet. There he would twist my body into a pretzel he proudly called "the figure four hold," which shut off my ability to breathe or even move a muscle. It also hurt like a torture rack, and naturally, I cried. All of this crying earned only more scorn.

"You girl," he scoffed at me—his ultimate insult.

He figured that since everything frightened me, he might as well get some amusement out of that too. In our shared bedroom he would tell scary stories about the headless horseman until I cried. He also became the mad puppeteer of the "spider hand" from the top bunk. Looking up in the dark, I would see an undulating five-fingered tarantula descending toward my head. I would shriek until Mom entered the room, switching on the light.

Gordon now snored sweetly, his hand hanging benignly over the side of the bunk.

"It's him," I insisted, "he's scaring me with his hand."

"Gordon?"

"Huh-uhh? Wha's a matter? I'm tryin' to sleep."

"See?" Mom would say. "Your brother's been asleep and now you woke him up. I think your imagination has become overactive again. Don't you?"

"No!" I insisted. But it was all useless.

Gordon's haunting of me just wouldn't end. He loved to hide behind doors in the dark whenever I got up in the night to go to the bathroom. As I returned, he would suddenly leap out. Of course, I would scream, providing great amusement. Then, as he switched on the lights, I would—what else—cry tears of relief, seeing that he was not the headless horseman, just my demon-possessed brother. More scorn.

It was no less an ordeal when he decided *not* to scare me. I scared myself enough thinking that he might be lurking in every shadow. "Gordon, are you there?" I would repeat all the way back to the bedroom. Finding him asleep—if I could trust appearances—I would resist an urge to drive a wooden stake through his heart.

Mom provided a saving grace for me. A very pretty redhead with a ready smile and a vivacious, hospitable presence, she gave the necessary affection to all seven of her offspring. On occasion I would manage to work my way through the crowd to rat effectively to her about Gordon's torments. It would earn him a royal chewing-out, and Griz would often pile on with a restriction. It could provide a serious inconvenience for Gordy.

He would corner me later, sneering, "You hopeless, tattletale baby. What is the matter with you?" As he spoke, he shook his head slowly, as if I had some dread disease.

The cumulative effect of this treatment led to my trying to kill him with a three-pound rock when I was nine and he was eleven. We had been forced by Dad to do yard work together. Gordon had bent over to drink out of a garden hose, leaving the back of his head unprotected. The next thing I knew the rock had found its way into my hands, poised itself above his head, ready to smash downward and end the torment of living with him. The Bible illustration of Cain and Abel flashed before my eyes. Pondering the deeper significance of sin is not effective in violent situations. Gordon, of course, never suffered such qualms.

He looked up to see the rock held ineptly above his head. His facial muscles became frozen as an improbable drop of water slid from the corner of his mouth to the ground. The spouting hose dropped from his hand with a slosh.

I should have killed him when his head was turned, I thought. *Now I will have to endure this endless look of scorn, and who knows what else?*

Breaking from his trance, he lunged upward, snatching the rock from my hands and throwing it aside. "What are you doing? You baby!" he spit. Then he took a few steps in one direction, stopped, scratched his head, took a few steps the other way, stopped again, and finally walked a complete circle before asking, "What *is* the matter with you?"

I do remember that look on his face. An expression of puzzled admiration, as if for the first time I had earned the status of partial human being in his eyes. Of course, to his way of thinking, I still had a long way to go.

Perhaps if I drew blood next time?

As Gordon entered junior high, Griz moved the family to St. Helens, Oregon, just north of Portland. There, Gordon found his first summer job—a job was a foreign idea invading my inner universe. He became a strawberry picker for a contract foreman. The foreman happened to be a member of Dad's new congregation. I recall him as a large, dull-faced man who summoned to mind the Jolly Green Giant. I do not mean to say that he was green or dressed in corn shucks, but he looked as if peas, beans, and berries were the only things that could put a gleam in his eye. A dirt-farmer type. I instantly felt that I would not do well around this man.

Not so with Gordon. I remember that he got up regularly before daylight, boarded a bus, and returned home near dark—none of which appealed to me in the slightest. *What a waste of summer,* I thought. I preferred to stay home and read, or perhaps visit the public swimming pool across the street for the mere price of a quarter. After a few weeks of this, Dad ordered me off my lazy behind to earn my swimming pool quarters in the strawberry fields with my brother.

Getting out of bed before daylight seemed almost impossible. Of course, Gordon had already gotten up, dressed, breakfasted, and waited for the bus—before I could *say* strawberry. The bus driver honked several times for me. Mother motioned for him to wait while I found my jacket, then my sack lunch, then my glasses, then my handkerchief—all of which I had conveniently misplaced. Losing the appeal of a last minute whine at the door, I finally boarded the loathed bus.

Gordon sat stonily, not acknowledging my inferior presence. I knew better than to sit anywhere near him. I decided to practice my pew sleeping skills and curled up in the rear of the bus, hoping not to be found when the time for real work came.

No such luck. The bus driver shooed me out the door as the other workers unloaded at the strawberry field just after dawn. I took my impossibly cold lunch sack and accepted a strawberry carrier from the Jolly Green Giant—who informed me that my brother was the top picker in his field, filling forty carriers a day. "That's ten bucks! Good money for a kid. Fifty bucks a week, I tell ya. You oughta be like your brother."

I'd rather eat dead possum guts.

I took my place between the dewy leaves of what seemed to be an endless row of mindlessly identical strawberry plants. One plant after the other, green leaves covering clusters of ripe and ripening berries, stretching for miles and miles and miles without end! *How could farmers be so cruel to make fields of such size?* I lamented.

By the time I had oriented myself to the impossibility of the task, all the other pickers were already working ten feet down their rows ahead of me. They had found a way to concentrate on the berries in front of them instead of contemplating the whole field. Their technique involved sharing tidbits of small-town gossip as they went. *What am I doing here?* I thought.

I would simply have to find my own way. Reaching beneath the green cluster of leaves before me, I picked a single ripe berry, holding it up to the morning sun for inspection. What a revelation. The color and texture of its shocking red skin seemed truly exquisite. I marvelled at those tiny seeds situated so perfectly in each delicate strawberry dimple. How could such a miracle occur in nature? Forty carriers a day are picked by fools like Gordon, I reasoned; only God can make a unique berry like this.

My mouth began to water. Our large family could ill afford such delicacies at table, with seven kids and all. Now

I sat in a field of countless delights. This particular work of God seemed destined for my mouth.

Then I noticed Gordon. Beyond belief, he had already moved three times farther down his row than any of the other pickers. He didn't squat or sit. He bent his back at a totally inhuman angle, one which would have rendered me wheelchair-bound in five minutes. He picked with both hands like a machine, grabbing fistful of berries like he was mad at them or something. He didn't appreciate a single one of those beautiful delicacies; he just mashed them and dumped them without looking. Mashing, dumping, mashing, dumping. Forty carriers of mutilated berries—that was his secret.

"You're mashing the berries!" I called after him.

"They're going to the jelly factory, idiot!" he explained. He spoke without looking at me, as if my comment hadn't deserved breaking his robot stride.

I decided then and there that I would be the one picker in the field to cherish the individuality of each God-created berry. This would be my special mission. Another one went into my mouth.

By the end of the day I had moved perhaps five or ten feet. There were no more pickers in my field. Others had come to finish my row, asked to do so by the good church-going foreman, who scowled at me and drove me by car to catch up to the rest of the crew—now vanished over the infinite strawberry horizon.

Realizing that I had accumulated little more than half a carrier of produce, equalling twelve-and-a-half-cents in pay—a half day at the swimming pool—I decided that this indignity was unfair to the very special berries in my care. They deserved more. I would have to help these natural wonders achieve their full potential. So, sitting in another impossibly long row, I employed the decorator's skill. I gave my berries a bit of soil in the bottom of the carrier so that they could be lifted up and properly displayed on top where they belonged. Of course, a few of them had lost their luster after spending a full day cut off from the vine. It is fair to say they had wilted. No matter; they were berries for God.

Triumphantly, I turned in my carrier at the end of the day, "Twenty-five cents, please."

It was the most disgraceful carrier of strawberries that foreman had ever seen, or so he told my parents later. By his account, it tripled the weight of any other cheated load he had ever confiscated.

"Some people have actually gotten away with a little dirt," he said, "but your son's carrier was more than half full of it!"

He seemed duty-bound, to God and the honorable name of the church, to report the full details of my sin. With a look intended to dismiss me from the human race and a sermon designed to send me straight to hell without supper, he fired me, in front of Mom and Griz, and requested that I never again return to his strawberry fields. I never did.

The last I saw of Gordon, he rode off with the Jolly Green Giant in a pickup truck to join a group of commercial pickers harvesting premium berries for roadside fruit stands at twice the ordinary pay. I learned later that Gordon was the youngest member ever drafted into this elite force of migrant, strawberry-picking commandos. The look he gave me as he disappeared into the mists of glory seemed to come from another entire universe, one where he lived and breathed and I would never enter.

Later, as I sunned myself at the public swimming pool, it occurred to me that I had achieved in shame about the same measure of notoriety Gordon had achieved through hard work. A small smile played in the corners of my mind. I couldn't help it. It is difficult to explain, and even more difficult to justify, but I felt immensely pleased to have made my mark in the opposite direction from him.

I didn't work with Gordon again until years later, as he prepared to enter the eleventh grade and I the ninth. Griz again moved our family to a new parsonage, in Hermiston, a town of five thousand inhabitants among the sage and wheat fields of eastern Oregon, thirty miles from Pendleton. A building contractor in the new community—a deacon who knew nothing of the strawberry fields—soon invited the preacher's boys to work on homesites he developed on the edge of town.

Gordon snorted his disgust and told the man outright that I was as worthless as a lame sister at any form of real work. But Griz intervened as both father and pastor, insisting that his boys be hired together or not at all. Time had passed, and I had done some growing, he explained. I am sure he hoped against hope that some of Gordon's industriousness would at last rub off on me.

But Gordon didn't believe in second chances. At least not for inferior specimens like me. He had tested and tried me every way imaginable and found me wanting the basic ingredients of manhood. End of story.

Secretly, I took the challenge in his indictment. If I had created the infamous mark of shame in the strawberry fields, I thought, then by golly, now I would do the impossible and erase it.

Gordon soon complicated my resolve, however. Born with spurs on and wanting to join a high school rodeo club, he made an agreement with the contractor behind my back. They agreed that the two of us would work not for wages but for possession of an old mountain saddle Gordon had spotted languishing in the contractor's barn.

When Gordy proudly announced the deal at the family supper table, my hopes slipped into a pit of cow dung. I cared less than zero for the saddle. I wanted money for new clothes to impress my new friends in the new town.

I did my best to hide any reaction at all, realizing that if I took this challenge from Gordon, it might prove to be the shame eraser I needed to gain back my humanity in his eyes. I surprised him and agreed that if he worked for half of the saddle, I would work for the other half, and after that, we could saw it in two—or he could work it off with me, whichever seemed best.

Gordon agreed that it seemed best to buy the other half rather than hack it up.

With this incident I began to compete on a more level playing field with him . . . well, at least I had made a tentative start. I soon suffered a setback—one that would punish me for years to come.

During my first week at Bull "pup" Junior High—the high school mascot was a bulldog; our diminutive version reminded us constantly of our inferior status—a towering five-foot-ten bully followed me home and began to taunt me on the front lawn of the parsonage. Helplessly cornered, I turned toward the house, noticing my preacher-dad Griz watching through the picture window. "Help," I signaled, using my best pantomime of Gomer Pyle. But I knew better. Griz would want me to stand up to the bully for my own good. He no doubt saw this as another of life's hard lessons, like summer jobs and other challenges I refused to face. I would never learn to handle such matters if he always bailed me out.

Where is Mom? I prayed, turning back toward the insulting brute. She could be counted on at times like these. Her softness, tenderness, and sympathy created an oasis of sanity for me. She also had a way of persuading Griz that his view of the crisis was purely provincial. But no, God had arranged for her absence on this day, because He quite possibly hated me.

The bully was taller. He outweighed me. His fists were larger and arms longer than mine. His foul mouth twisted and sneered one profanity after another across the parsonage lawn. That's when I noticed his breath. Only a ninth grader, this Philistine smoked cigarettes. Furthermore, he had come close enough so that I could read the brand through his shirtsleeve—Marlboro. The black tips of real whiskers grew on his upper lip and chin. This Neanderthal must have flunked sixteen grades. In a fair world, I thought, guys with whiskers would never be allowed to punch guys like me with glasses and peach fuzz.

"Stay out of our yard," I croaked as he stepped menacingly forward.

"Who's gonna make me?"

Again, I glanced at Griz as if to say, "Are you going to put up with this?" Dad crossed his grizzly arms and scowled. I could read signals from the dugout—bases loaded, two out, full count, and it was up to me to swing away. I knew Dad was angry with me for taking the verbal abuse, as angry as he might have been at the bully for dishing it out. I had no refuge. A good, sound thrashing lay before me—and behind me. Somewhere in the middle, I remained paralyzed.

In fairness, Dad had taught both Gordon and me to use our fists. A former military boxer, he had sparred with us using eight-ounce boxing gloves so that we would not be defenseless at times like this. He didn't believe in letting a bully use us as a doormat simply because we were preacher's kids. Furthermore, he practiced what he preached. I had seen him manhandle more than one heckler in my time. However, under the pressure of the moment I converted to the other version of Christianity—"Love thine enemies." I did not want to stand and fight. Call me quitter, crybaby, a girl, whatever, I had not the fortitude to shed blood. Especially not mine. I backed down.

In a flurry of motion, Gordon burst from the house behind me. Evidently he had arrived home from Bulldog High and had entered the house from the backyard. Seeing my disgraceful dodge, he raced past me across the lawn and before my incredulous eyes, actually reached up to smack the bully in the face. They promptly began duking it out in the street.

I did not want my brother to do this; I wanted Griz to intervene. But Gordon had done it without a moment's hesitation—before I could make up my mind about the universal, moral, and practical significance of human violence. Such numbing thoughts had actually run through my mind as the bully had called me every name in his filthy vocabulary.

Wham! Bam! I can still see Gordon's nose bleeding from the rain of blows that should have landed on me. At the end of the fight, which ended in a draw, the bully said, "OK, Gordon. I thought you were nothing but a wimpy preacher's kid, but you're all right. It's your brother there who's a yellow-bellied coward." He promised to look for me around town.

Gordon never said a word to me about it but went back into the house, washed up, and continued his routines as if nothing had happened.

A huge black *F* entered my gradebook of shame.

The following fall was the first season our family hunted the larger member of the deer family: the *wapiti*, or elk. The Blue Mountains of eastern Oregon provided abundant herds of these magnificent animals. For this reason, moving to that region of the state had long been at the top of Griz's wish list.

On our first elk hunting experience, Dad placed Gordon and me together on a rocky point to watch for bulls while he hunted through a stand of timber below us. Gordon had the only gun between us. I still lacked adequate shooting skills at the time and had come along to learn about this new kind of hunting. I manned a pair of binoculars.

To our great excitement, a spike bull emerged from the timberline far below our stand. Dad had evidently spooked it into the open. I breathlessly watched through the binoculars as Gordon aimed his Enfield .30-06 with buckhorn sights for the kill. *Blam!* I could see a dark patch appear just behind the animal's shoulder, but to our amazement the bull walked on as if nothing had happened.

"What's going on?" Gordon rasped, firing again. Again, I saw another impact behind the shoulder. This time the animal stopped. A third broadside brought him down. After we had scrambled down the steep slope to his side, a fourth shot was necessary to finally kill the animal.

Gordon was amazed and very angry with himself. For the first time in his life he had not brought an animal down with one quick killing shot. As he field-dressed the elk, he examined its wounds to understand his mistake. Unraveling the mystery, he explained it to me. He pointed up at the rock where we had been sitting, suddenly realizing just how steep the shooting angle had been. The elk had appeared broadside to us from our perch on the rocky point but the steep grade had actually presented an illusion to our eyes. The vital organs, normally located just behind the shoulder on level ground, had in this case been high, just under the backbone.

"Next time I have a shot like this," Gordon said as he continued to skin the young bull, "I'll aim high and he'll go down the first time. No suffering."

I took precise mental notes.

Just after the season ended, the entire nation received word of the work of another unlikely, yet incredible, marksman; one who had apparently learned his downhill shooting lessons better than could be believed. On November 22, 1963, while waiting for Algebra class to begin, I heard the announcement over the school intercom system that John F. Kennedy had been killed by an assassin's bullet. A deep silence that would not go away descended in the hallways and classrooms. Only weeping and the occasional outbreak of hysterical sobbing punctuated the dead air until another announcement crackled through the speaker box, closing classes for the day.

I walked a tree-lined Hermiston lane to our parsonage not knowing what to think or feel, only calculating that if a presidential assassination was possible, perhaps nuclear war was possible too. I placed each foot with dread on the sidewalk, as if it were a rug that might be jerked out from under me.

Reaching the house, I received my second world-changing shock of the day; Griz had rented a TV set, installing it in the basement to watch the important events of national mourning over the president's death. This was the first time such an instrument of evil had been allowed into our house.

"It's all in controlling the knob," he explained. "This TV is for watching serious news events. Period. None of this other trashy stuff that comes through the 'boob tube.' Not in my house."

Within weeks he had made one fatal exception to his own absolute rule. It was now religiously correct for the preacher and his boys to watch the upcoming holiday bowl games, he decided, and perhaps an NFL game or two, but nothing else. In a home with four non-football-fanatic females, he met an immediate wall of yammering about fairness. By lusting to watch football, Griz eventually had his fingers pried from the TV channel selector entirely. The girls overwhelmed him with the number of "decent" forms of entertainment that appealed to their sensibilities.

In effect, Dad traded "Leave it to Beaver," "I Love Lucy," and "Petticoat Junction" for the opportunity to watch Michigan play USC. In the long run, he traded much more than that.

Once defeated on the overarching issue, TV technology itself overwhelmed the household with its viewing choices. Us kids, heretofore starved for the sounds and images of our culture, had acquired no criteria for choosing well. With merely our appetites as guides, we chose very badly indeed. The only question among the socially hungry crowd in the basement—once our parents had left the room—was "who got there first" to establish control over the knob. After that, Griz's offspring resembled bear cubs in a garbage dump; sampling anything and everything out of sheer curiosity. Thus, our family played catch-up to America at the cost of an incalculable innocence.

In my fourteenth year, Gordon's sixteenth, I had grown taller than him and gained the advantage of having the longer arms between us. This physical change tilted the balance of perceived power in my favor, at least in the not-so-subtle opinions of our assertive younger siblings. Meanwhile, in the presence of this new tension, I secretly stood before every mirror in the house trying to flex a visible bicep. I knew muscles should come along any day now, accompanying the new height and perhaps glorifying my wimpy preacher's kid existence.

One hot summer day the tension became too much. Gordon and I exploded into a fist fight while carrying groceries to the house for Mom.

"Stop it right now, boys!" she screeched.

To no avail. Gordon invited me to put on the eight-ounce boxing gloves Dad kept in the basement "so we can hit as hard as we want and finish this on the back lawn right now," he challenged.

"OK," I agreed.

Mom must have figured that boxing gloves would reduce the contest to the level of a pillow fight, and so it was allowed to happen—and I almost erased my *F* mark of shame with one lucky punch. Griz bore witness from the bedroom window to the only knockout his number one son is known to have suffered. As we danced around and pawed the air, I delivered a simple left jab, but it landed straight on Gordon's jaw as he swung a round-house right. *Whack!* To my complete surprise, it connected like a pile driver. His head snapped back and he keeled over, eyes rolled up, all white and funny looking.

According to Gordon's account I had found his Achille's heel, his "glass jaw." He claimed that he could take a punch anywhere but on that particular part of his face. As the years went by Gordon continued to retell the story, adding the detail that I had gone on to ruin a perfectly good fight by throwing off my boxing gloves, grabbing his senseless head, and pleading, "No, no, no, Gordy, please don't die," as he lay spread-eagle on the lawn.

So much for my killer instinct.

Late in the summer of '64, Gordon had begun to tell tales around the dinner table of a nearby ranch where he and his cowboy buddies practiced bull riding. It had become a daily routine for these would-be rodeo stars. After finishing a twelve-hour shift of harvesting Hermiston watermelons, they would drive an old rusty pickup over to the arena and put in an hour or two of practice on an honest-to-goodness bull.

The key to my ear in this description was the use of the singular word *bull*—which I heard somewhat in the metaphorical sense as well. While the rest of the family listened to his tale with proper awe and near worship, I perceived that Gordon and his buddies were wearing this animal down in the course of an evening. Inquiring about the time of day they engaged in their bold activity, I suggested that I might drive Griz's four-banger out to watch them since I had recently acquired my driving permit.

Proper response as far as Gordon was concerned. "Fine," he said, "do it."

I did.

"Come on," Gordon challenged as I sat on the fence. "Come take a whirl on this bull."

"Naw, you guys go on ahead."

After thirty minutes of watching, as I had suspected, the animal lost its real bucking power. The rides became more manageable. I walked across the arena announcing that I wanted to ride.

Even knowing that the animal was not fresh, Gordon seemed ready to congratulate me for courage. Any kind of bravado had been an undiscovered quality in my life so far. He eagerly strapped his spurs on me, gave me his riding glove, and explained the details of a bull rig. Then he demonstrated the correct way to spur to make points for the judges as the chute was opened.

"Aw, forget spurring," he admonished. "The main thing in bull riding is just to stay on."

I mounted the animal, inserted a gloved hand into the rope, and yelled, "Let 'er rip!"

Gordon shook his head. "Go for it," he said to the chute crew.

They opened the chute and the bull made two or three feeble attempts to dislodge me as I spurred like a windmill. "Come on, bull, what kind of animal are you?" I screamed.

The weary bull began trotting harmlessly around the arena. I continued to spur and challenge him to throw me, knowing that it would not be likely. Finally, I leaped from his back in mock disgust. Removing the gloves, I slapped the animal across his weary haunches before walking past Gordon and into the jeep.

"You're not the only cowboy on the range," I said. "I just rode that so-called bull of yours to a standstill."

The comment must have struck a cowboy nerve. A roar of laughter erupted from Gordon and his buddies. I played it to the hilt, firing the jeep's engine and cutting a dusty one-eighty in the barnyard before driving off into the sunset.

That night at the supper table Gordon elaborated on my bull ride as if it had been legitimate. "He rode that bull to a standstill," he boasted on my behalf, slyly repeating my own line of braggadocio: "I guess I'm not the only cowboy on the range."

Suckered by my own pride, I let his words stand without even a modest correction. The story became a bogus part of family lore that proved to be a mistake. Everyone's expectations of me grew unrealistically high. Worse than that, knowing Gordon as I did, he would soon demand that I live up to my legend. I could feel my day of reckoning coming.

Gordon graduated from Bulldog High School with the class of '65 and entered a community college in Pendleton, thirty miles from home. He moved into an apartment near the campus with a few of his cowboy buddies who joined him in forming a college rodeo club.

Meanwhile, I entered my junior year at high school and a new phase of competition with him in English Composition. This contest *in absentia* began when I heard my name called for roll.

"Here," I answered.

Mr. Smith, bald as a cue ball and just as unfuzzy,

acclaimed to be "the most demanding brain-tyrant in Bull-dog history," looked at me over his reading glasses.

"Are you any relation to Gordon?"

"Yeah, we're brothers." I felt two opposite things in admitting my kinship here. First, I felt backup. If it ever came to a fight I liked the idea of having a big brother. However, in matters of scholarship, I wanted to be on my own. Here on my first day with Gordon away at college, I found that he threw a thirty-mile shadow.

Until that moment all I knew of Gordon's writing ability was that he had the worst penmanship on the planet. It resembled the tracks of a startled band of turkeys in the snow, though somewhat less readable. *All* of his personal habits were accomplished with about the same disdain, like the way he maintained his bedroom, decorated with boots and Levi's-adhering-to-cow-dung flung in random piles. To my complete surprise, however, I now learned that he had been graded for something other than neatness in Mr. Smith's elite class.

"Your brother was one of the most brilliant students I have ever taught in here," Smith explained with a wilting gaze. "His writing samples exhibited the natural instincts of writers like Hemingway. He earned straight As from me. Are you *that* good?"

I was stunned. And burned. I had no idea if I was that good. Come to think of it, probably not. For a moment I entered "the twilight zone," taken back to a strawberry field where Gordon's impossibly bent back vanished into the mists of glory ahead of me. He beat me at everything. The difference between strawberries and writing lay in the fact that in writing I wanted desperately to be better than him. However, it appeared that the deck of natural talent had been stacked against me by a God who had decided that since I was a crybaby, He too would enjoy Himself and give me something to cry about.

Swallowing my fear, including a proper fear of God, I answered in a newfound rebellious voice. "Maybe we'll see if he's as good as me."

Smith stared blankly over his reading glasses for a long moment. Then his face tensed into a vulturelike smile. The old cue ball liked the answer, but his ultimate verdict about my talent became indelibly inscribed upon a report card: B's and C's. Nothing special.

Along about mid-semester Gordon surprised the family by dropping out of college to join the Army. Vietnam called him to do his duty for America, as his father had done before him in World War II. He explained it as simply as that. He had become what Griz called "gung-ho," which meant putting one's patriotic heart before one's sensible head. Admirable, but not always advisable; especially since a bunch of Washington bureaucrats couldn't decide if this was a real war or just a police action. Meanwhile, we kept seeing those body counts on the six o'clock news.

Months later Gordon flew home from boot camp. He had changed, I thought. Actually, it seemed he had hardened like cement, becoming more himself: more determined, more cocksure, more of an absolutist.

He smoked in the backyard—a big shock. None of

Griz's children had openly defied his behavioral standards. The last time I had smoked at the age of nine, it had resulted in a thrashing worth several sins. The rest of us looked at one another as Gordon puffed, waiting for the hand of judgment to fall. Dad said nothing, and a pall of confusion seemed to descend on the household. Gordon, in his military uniform, had asserted a foreign authority against the one authority we had all accepted without question.

I wondered what this might have to do with becoming a man.

Mysteriously, during his brief furlough, Gordon motioned me one day into the backyard and into the Willys four-banger.

"Where are we going?"

"You'll see. Just get in."

He drove east across the wheat and sage country to a remote basalt cliff directly above the Columbia River, several miles into the backwaters of McNary Dam.

"What are we doing here?"

"A lesson in life," Gordon said, stripping to his shorts and revealing that in a few short months his body had become a mass of well-proportioned muscle. Intimidating to say the least; I still nursed that first bicep, praying for a truly worthy hormone to enter my bloodstream.

"Take off your clothes and dive in," he said. "Come on, I'll teach you something."

I choked. A screaming, weak-kneed, pleading crybaby took over my brain, jerking the fear-controls like a child with a Tonka Truck. Nothing could drag me closer than ten feet to the edge of this deathtrap. It remained unthinkable that I would throw myself indiscriminately into the cold gray depths of the Columbia River from a height of sixty or seventy feet. Not on your life. Not for manhood. Not even for the adoration of every screaming high school cheerleader in eastern Oregon.

He positioned himself on his toes on the cliff's edge, arms stretched to either side. "Swan dive," he announced.

Clearing my throat in order to keep my voice as near to normal as possible—though it quickly got away from me—I bleated, "This is how paraplegics are made."

He turned and scowled at me for my poor taste and timing. After all, he was the one on the line here. "No, little brother," he said, "this is how you die. From this height, you hit a rock and it's all over." Then he stepped away from the cliff, toward me. His face twisted into that puzzled, disbelieving look he always gave just before saying, *"You're so naive!"*

"Don't you get it?" he said. "This is not about dying, it's about living. No one can really live as long as they fear death. Look it in the face."

Questions of death, my own or Gordon's, I intended to keep on hold in my mind until approximately my one hundred and thirty-third birthday, or thereafter. On my private fear scale, death scored off the chart. So what if Gordon thought that I didn't know how to live. That was only his opinion.

"Can we just go back now and not do this?" I said.

He sighed wearily. "Come over here."

"I don't want to come over there."

"Come here, you nit!" he suddenly roared, leaping at me like a pouncing lion. He gripped my arm in his berry-mashing fingers and drug me struggling like a trapped deer to the cliff's edge. "I'm not going to throw you over!" he yelled. "Stand still!"

Clinging to the hope that he remained a man of his word even after graduating from boot camp, I swallowed hard, trying to relax, shuddering, my knees sagging involuntarily. I began to hyperventilate.

"Get a hold on yourself," he said. His fingers did not relax their bruising grip on my arm. He knew I would bolt for the jeep at the first opportunity. "You think I'm not scared?" he rasped. "Everybody's scared. So what? Babies are scared. Women are scared. But men have to overcome it. Look at me."

I did. I saw the brother who wouldn't cry when Griz whipped him. I saw the guy who swam icy rivers as I turned blue on the shore. I saw his five fingered tarantula descending toward my head from the top bunk in the dark. Nothing had basically changed between us, even though now he had become a crew cut Army private with two dozen maturing, almost-whiskers on his cheek. His jaw muscles worked beneath that stubble like a pump; his eyes glistened with his most determined blue-eyed brother stare.

"The difference between you and me," he said, "is that I have decided that I will not let fear keep me from doing anything—*anything* I decide to do. At boot camp they put me in a gas chamber and turned on the gas, then threw in a gas mask. I had to control my fear to be able to put on the mask and breathe again. You should have seen the other guys, coughing and screaming. Not me. I used my willpower. Remember when I fought the bully? I knew he'd get in a few punches, but did that stop me? No. I didn't care. I did my damage. He couldn't beat me because I wouldn't quit and he knew it. He quit." He tapped the index finger of his free hand against his temple. "Willpower. This is not about fear. It's about willpower. Now, I *will* dive from this cliff then I want you to follow me. If you don't, you'll never amount to anything. Now, for once in your life, I want you to shut off your stupid fear and use your willpower to do what any real man would do."

He unleashed my arm with a violent shrug and I stumbled backward.

Turning to the cliff, he spread his arms artfully, staring down at the gray backwater. "All anybody needs is seven feet of water," he explained.

Oh sure, I thought, *you fall seventy feet like a rock and all you need is seven feet of water? Brilliant!*

"There's at least seven feet down there," he mused. "As soon as you hit, what you do is lift your head and hands like this and you'll shoot to the surface. See?"

Sure, like magic.

With that, he spread his arms wide and raised himself on tiptoe, legs together, head up, eyes open. Checking the distance one more time, he willed himself into a breathtaking arc toward the water.

I leaped forward on my hands and knees, crawling to the cliff's edge. Looking over, I could see him holding a perfect swan dive as he watched the water rush toward him, timing his head-tuck for the moment of impact. His body disappeared with a splash, only to reappear seconds later like a cork, twenty feet beyond the point of entry. His method resulted exactly as he had predicted. Willpower worked—at least for him.

"Whew!" he exulted, swinging his fists wildly over his head. "Come on, do it! *Do it*, you nit!"

In that moment it seemed to me that the differences between Gordon and me were as deep as that chasm above the water. I did not have his willpower. I would never have it. Furthermore, I did not want to have it. If I could not be a man by his rules, then fine; I would be a man by some other rule.

As Gordon began to scale the cliff toward me, I backed away toward the jeep, wiping fiercely at a couple of tears I didn't even have the willpower to stop.

On the long drive home through the sage and wheat country, Gordon's silence seemed to reveal an inner struggle. Finally he spoke, after reaching an uneasy summation. "If you don't stay in school . . . and keep your grades up—I mean, if you do something stupid like lose your college deferment and let them draft you, I swear I'll get my gun and shoot you myself!"

Strangely, I sensed a new attitude here. He acted angry, but the anger seemed to have driven him in the right direction where I was concerned. He seemed to be accepting me, even with my too many fears.

Though it hurt my pride, I agreed with his verdict of my character that day. Nothing would have pleased me more than to have believed in myself enough to promise him then and there that I would grow out of this fear and follow him in the path of manhood someday. But I could not do that, no matter how unmanly I seemed. In my inner world fear had always loomed larger than pride, anyway.

By this time in my life, watching the nightly TV news reports from Vietnam, I knew that the violent realities of the world we shared paralyzed me, mind and soul. In my view, Gordon could face death on the cliff, or in Vietnam. I would do anything and everything to avoid it.

Gordon left for the battlefields as I began my senior year in high school. I tried to hide myself in personal pursuits, but life would not allow it. It rarely does. The town bully, the Philistine Gordon had fought after I had backed down—this same God-ordained mouthpiece of putrefaction—began to make my life miserable again at every turn.

"Where's your big brother now, preacher's boy? You gonna hide behind Momma's skirts? Are ya? Huh, yellow-belly? Huh?"

Truthfully, I did hide behind my mother's skirts. My mother became my main source of sanity during this shameful year. I avoided every social excursion in town out of fear of meeting up with the bully. No more skating rink, after school clubs, sporting events, or dates. Instead, I buried myself in the toughest math and science courses I could find. Driving Dad's yellow jeep directly to and from school, no detours. I'd hit the books at home until bedtime, then start the routine all over again the next day. I worked weekends feeding milk bottles into a power washing machine at a local dairy. I enjoyed the long hours of solitude in that hot, steamy room: sweating, manhandling those crated-bottles, venting frustrations, returning home late at night. I would usually find Mom sitting up, reading or knitting. My younger brother and sisters would all be asleep. This became my treasured time. Mom would rub my feet and we would talk.

"Gordy wrote this week."

"Oh yeah?" His shadow reached me again—this time, over a distance of 7,000 miles.

"He's in the hospital. Said it's not serious but he took some shrapnel in the face."

I couldn't comprehend it. War's realities were a part of that separate universe where Gordon lived.

Midway through the year, I began to realize that I had not drawn a single free breath since Gordon left town. Soon I would be leaving home myself, choosing a college, taking a career direction. I began to ask myself how I could leave the bully business undone. It would follow me—at least in my mind it would—reminding me of my real failure. Somehow I would have to remove the albatross from around my neck.

During deer season 1967, I saw Griz miss a large mule deer buck in a herd of five. We spooked the animals and his running shot was ill-timed. On the final day of the season I returned to the area alone and tracked the herd again through a fresh snow, killing a trophy animal for the family larder. I brought its large four point rack home and proudly mounted it on the carport.

"A running shot at three hundred yards," I boasted for any who would listen. With Gordon in Vietnam, my words rang in the house like a dozen dropped marshmallows.

A few weeks later I bagged the 1967 bull elk that marked me as the family "hunter of the year." Dad had been duly impressed; "Old Dead Eye!" he had enthused.

During our drive home from the Blue Mountains, we talked somberly of Gordon's recent letters outlining dangerous reconnaissance missions behind enemy lines.

As the school year drew to a close, springtime must have launched that long-awaited hormone into my bloodstream. What indicates such a biological change? When the bull elk bugles, it signals the start of mating season. When the bucks lower their antlers to fight, you know they are in the rut. When a puny preacher's kid, in a moment of apparent insanity, walks a bully's girlfriend down the hall, sap must be running in the trees somewhere.

The two of us arrived blissfully at her locker, which was next to his, and from the look on his face I figured that 666 antichrist profanities reached critical mass inside his skull. Unable to utter a sound, the bully gazed at me, the corners of his mouth twitching like severed lizard tails. His facial skin turned several shades toward the lower end of the rainbow until I feared he might suffer a heart attack. At any rate, the long-overdue fight was definitely on.

Word got out that we were meeting in the park immediately, and it became the main event for Bulldog High. In a school of less than five hundred students, I was told later that it was as if classes had been dismissed. The entire football team showed up, including the Bulldog Boosters, cheerleaders, and, of course, all the C, D, and F students. Even some local policemen pulled up in a squad car to watch this bully finally get his due. It had become common knowledge that my brother had fought this guy to protect me years ago. Now I had grown up and would defend myself.

As I approached the park with a growing crowd behind me, the punk threw his hot rod into a four-wheel skid near the entrance. Leaping from the driver's side he ran at me like a barnyard bull. As quickly as possible I dropped my two armloads of books, slung off my calf-length coat, pushed up the sleeves of my burgundy velour sweater, and rose to the balls of my tan Hushpuppies like a commando-preppie. After I had ducked several vicious punches, someone in the crowd suggested that I should remove my horn-rimmed glasses. I did, and tossed them behind me. Such gestures usually mean that "now the real fight will begin," but in my case, nothing escalated.

I bounced around, using everything Griz had taught me—well, at least the *defensive* part of it. I sparred, keeping damage down with long jabs and counterpunches. Unfortunately, none of them connected with the lucky one-punch power of that backyard fight with Gordon. After an interminable five minutes or so, my arms grew heavy. I became totally winded, and actually bored with the insanity of it all.

It is neither wise nor healthy to become bored in the middle of a three-year grudge match. But for me, the whole thing was already over. All I had needed to do was finally show the courage to face my tormentor. Finishing the fight would add nothing to the accomplishment for me. Furthermore, the more I boxed, the more I knew that I did not really have it in me to bash the guy. If he had placed his face on a tee and had asked for punishment, I would have said, "Ah, go on and live your life."

After a while, fewer and fewer punches were being thrown. Both of us circled one another, gasping, heaving, arms about as nimble as lead pipes. It appeared that I had frustrated his plans for what he thought might be a pushover fight. Hoping that this meant that now he would listen to reason, I asked, "Don't you think this is absurd?"

The question might have scored some kind of brilliant psychological damage if only I had kept my guard up. But in the real world of street fighting it is worse than absurd to shrug for emphasis. I shrugged, holding a silly little inquiring smile on my face.

Wham! The splintered cartilage that had once been my nose began bleeding measurable quarts per second. I bent over and grabbed my face in disbelief. The Neanderthal kicked my head like a football. I remember spinning through the air and not much else. Later I was told that he had subsequently jumped on my unconscious body, beating the back of my head with a fistful of metal rings. When the dismayed crowd finally ran the bully off, I stumbled home with a mild, feeling-not-so-mild, concussion.

The whole world had wanted me to be as good as my brother that day, and I had let them down. Most of all, because I had finally tried to defend myself, I had seriously let myself down. I had fought as if I lived on a planet of wimps. I told myself I deserved the beating. Recalling that I had actually asked him to consider the absurdity of violence, I mused, "Now there's a story they'll be telling their grandchildren in this town for decades." I wanted to disappear.

Then something truly frightening happened. The next morning I awoke different. Something had changed in the night. I had gone to sleep with a deep ache of shame and emotional pain in my chest, hurting me more than any of the bruises and cuts on my face. I had drifted to sleep feeling more alone than I had ever felt, but I awoke not quite knowing myself. A rage seethed inside with such power that I feared I might not be able to control it.

I went to the bathroom and washed my face, peering into the mirror through the swollen slits of my multicolored eyelids. Bruises, cuts, and welts covered my forehead and cheeks where heavy rings had found their mark. My nose was twice its normal size and still oozing blood. The only place on my face I had managed to adequately protect was my jaw. The back of my head was covered with welts from the beating I had taken after being kicked unconscious.

Suddenly, I didn't want to control the rage. I wanted to go to school. I imagined that bully going to his first period class, crowing about his superior street fighting ability, and something inside of me decided that he would not succeed in doing that in a million years. To his surprise, I would be there today, battered and bruised. I would look him up, like his worst nightmare, and teach him a lesson in front of the whole school that he would never forget. In my rage I promised myself—*promised*—that his face would carry the scars of our meeting for the rest of his life.

When Gordon had gone to Vietnam, I had inherited his old bedroom in the basement. I went to the closet and removed a pair of pointed-toed cowboy boots. I had not found the courage to wear them before now. My Hushpuppies went flying into a corner. The civilized slacks I usually wore were tossed aside in favor of a pair of blue jeans. My soft velour sweater, blood-soaked from the day before, was discarded for one of Gordon's old flannel shirts.

Then I went to a drawer and removed a short piece of rusted iron, a rounded segment that fit neatly and comfortably inside my hand. When my fingers closed over it, the bar nearly disappeared but my fist contained an entirely new level of power. I slammed it against my open hand to test its heft again. I had discovered the scrap metal a year before and had saved it for just such an occasion. Placing it in my pocket, I began to seethe.

No breakfast that morning. No books. No need. I had only one reason for going to school. I quietly left the house through the basement exit to ensure that I would not answer to Mom or Griz.

I drove Dad's yellow jeep across town as usual. At the front entrance of the school I parked and got out. My regular parking space was on the south side, but I wanted to be seen by the students who customarily gathered in the main hallway before class. They needed to meet the new me. Some of them had thought they were my friends; they had never been my friends. I was on my own. I didn't want defenders, I didn't want backup, and I didn't want my big brother fighting my fights ever again. All that brought me comfort was the secret weapon in my pocket, which would help me do some permanent damage.

As I walked toward the large glass doors of the school, the students reacted. The cheerleaders huddled in a corner, glancing over their shoulders at me, whispering busily among themselves. I looked so badly beaten they did not want to face me directly, or even acknowledge that they had watched the fight. To my pleasure a star lineman from the football team stepped forward to meet me at the door, holding it open.

"Man, what are you doing here? You look awful."

"Thanks," I said. Every sentence I spit back at him was full of venom and overloaded with profanities. "My face is nothin' compared to what you are about to see. Where's—?" and I called the bully by a perverted form of his name.

"He's got P.E. first period—you're really going to take him on again?"

"They will have to carry him out of here."

"Yahoo!" he shouted, and he was immediately joined by every other male student within hearing. "Man, you're all right," he said, slapping my back.

I liked the feel of it. Perhaps I had discovered the missing part of myself that would finally make me a man. Reaching into my pocket, I took the iron bar into my fist and pulled it out. My head felt like a furnace. I couldn't wait to get started.

Entering the gymnasium, I saw a few students standing in groups talking. I broke into a run, looking across their faces for my quarry, but he was not there.

"Where is he?" I called.

Some began to pull at me as I passed. "No, no, you're too late. Let it go. He's gone."

When I finally comprehended what they were saying, I stopped. "He ran? Who told him I was coming?"

The phys ed teacher had been watching me. He nodded toward his glass-enclosed office. "Come in here, son, I'll explain it to you." Incredibly, as he spoke, he wiped at a small bruise growing below his left eye. "The guy took a swing at me and I had the police arrest him," he explained as he placed a strong hand on my shoulder and escorted me into the gymnasium office. "It's over. We're sending him to a juvenile offender program. You won't be seeing him in this town again."

The violent head of steam I had built found no outlet. I felt cheated, deflated. It had all happened too abruptly, like surging toward a locked door and having it opened from the other side just before impact. After three years of sheer torment, could it end like this—not with revenge but with an intervention that had nothing to do with me?

As I mentally stumbled through this question, a small feeling of relief began to tickle inside, in spite of myself. I realized that I could return to normal. This other part of me felt glad that I had not taken revenge. It was the piece of my soul that belonged to the Sunday school Scriptures: "Love thine enemies, do good to those who hate you. Forgive and you shall be forgiven." But how could I take comfort in them anymore? This was not Sunday school, it was the real world. Out here, the religious part of me had proven to be nothing but a coward. I was not a true Christian who turned the other cheek out of strength and love; I ran and hid from conflict out of plain old fear.

"Did you know how troubled his home is?"

The voice of the P.E. teacher brought me back to the present. "No," I said numbly, taking a seat unsteadily in front of his desk—not that it had been offered.

"It's a sad case," he went on, stretching back in his chair, folding his hands thoughtfully behind his closely cropped head of hair. "We've known about it for some time around here. We knew he was a time bomb. I know this may not mean much to you right now because you are still pretty banged up, but his stepdad beats his mom severely. He has had to intervene more than once to protect his mom until the police arrived at their house. Just a few weeks ago he beat his dad up. He and his mom keep a gun at the door now in case he tries to come back. This was a very troubled kid who took his frustrations out on you. We're just real sorry you got in the middle of it." He rubbed his growing black eye. "I got in the middle of it too, I guess. In the long run, neither of us should take this too personally."

I didn't know what to say. I was too busy wondering how this bully had managed to earn so much sympathy. Of course, the thought passed through my head accompanied by a flood of uncivilized adjectives.

After a pause, the phys ed teacher seemed to stumble across his counseling gem for me: "Say, your dad's a preacher, isn't he? Maybe you can understand this a little bit better than most: through this bad situation this guy is finally going to get the kind of help he needs to turn his life around. I think you're big enough to understand that, aren't you? Now, why don't you go on home and get some rest and come on back when you're feeling better, OK?"

I nodded absently.

Getting up to leave, I could almost feel my soul sinking into a well of isolation. What would it take, I wondered, before anyone realized how much trouble *I* was in? What in God's name would it take to turn *my* life around? Would I have to kill or maim someone before I earned sympathy? I placed the iron bar back into my pocket carefully, hoping that no one had seen it, and drove myself home for two days of recuperation.

Late spring. Just after graduation. I cruised the daffodil and buttercup lined Oregon highway riding a newly purchased Honda 305 Scrambler. I wished Gordon could have seen me. Bafflers removed from its raging dual pipes, the motorcycle growled like thunder across the now familiar wheat and sage land.

For the past year, news reports of Vietnam had shown more and more carnage. Gordon's letters home had contained mention of unthinkable night missions, belly-crawling behind enemy lines in the central highlands. He had spent time in a field hospital twice, only to return to fight again. On one mission he had seen most of his reconnaissance group carried away in body bags. Detecting a strange buildup of enemy forces, the Army had recently reassigned him to serve as a helicopter door gunner.

"This will be a real vacation," he wrote. "I'm looking

forward to flying missions over the beautiful Temple City of Hue."

Taking blind courage from his example, I had made a decision to buy my motorcycle against the objections of my parents. I had to make something happen, anything to change my life.

"Time for me to 'get it on,'" I had said to Griz and Mom with forced defiance. "No more hiding."

Roaring along now with the wind in my face, I tried to imagine the sensation of flying in the open door of a Huey helicopter, racing across some Asian rice paddy at low altitude. Following a faint jeep trail, I came to a dusty stop on a basalt cliff above the Columbia River, and parked the scrambler on the very spot where Gordon had dragged me, struggling like a trapped deer, more than a year before. Inspired by his real brushes with death and driven by my failure with the bully, I had decided the time had come to finish what Gordon had started here. Time to overcome fear with willpower. In the meantime, I had tried to bury my cowardice like a dead puppy, out of sight in the backyard of my brain.

Shedding my clothes, I dropped them piece by piece over the handlebars of my shiny new machine, trying not to contemplate the thing I had determined to do. *Don't think, just do,* I told myself. I removed the dark glasses and placed them on the seat of the scrambler and took a couple steps toward the cliff's edge.

Without warning the dead puppy burst back in on me. The whimpering, whining, simpering, crybaby terror. It howled for a hiding place. The ability of fear to erase all other thoughts and emotions in my brain had by no means diminished in a year. It erupted in a tight band of sweat around my brow. I could taste its curdling juices in my mouth. My stomach knotted, my breathing became shortened, my knees turned to rubber again. I knew that I still was not made like Gordon. I could not will myself through this.

Under these conditions I needed something stronger than willpower to drive me forward to the edge of that precipice. In a moment, I sensed what that stronger force might be. For me it would not be will, but emotion, and that emotion was anger. Perhaps even rage, the very red-eyed evil rage that had overcome me the morning after the beating. Only this time, instead of directing the rage at someone else, I would direct it at myself. *That's it,* I thought. A guy needs to hate himself to become a man.

Summoning all the fury I felt toward myself for allowing fear to drive me to cowardice, the piled up resentments against Gordon for his childhood torments, the frustration at Dad for his hardness, the wrath that had brewed since my humiliation by the bully, and anger at God for bringing me into this world of injustice—I sprinted forward, launching myself, fists flailing the air, through that dreaded distance that had separated two brothers for too long.

Splash.

I tore through the skin of the water into a gurgling, muffled, gray silence. Looking down, I descended toward the unmoved blackness below. *"Seven feet of water is all you need,"* Gordon had said. I was determined to descend to the very bottom, perhaps twenty or thirty feet down. As

I continued, bacterial silt, the abrasive agents of death, hung suspended in the deeper water. They brushed my legs as I passed, swirling in my wake. I imagined their eagerness, aroused by my passing, to obey their Maker and decompose flesh and bone. I gazed into the peaceful, impenetrable blackness below as it began to engulf me. Then my feet encountered reality, softly touching down on an icy stone. My legs bent like a soft spring, cushioning my descent, stopping it there. Toes holding to the rock's slimy crevices, I swirled my arms gently to hold myself below.

My lungs felt ready to shred, trying to contain the expanded air within them. My chest cramped, begging for relief. Looking up, a gray-orange glow promised that the surface still waited above. I loosened some air, watching a line of sparkling bubbles leap upward from my nose and mouth. Bright emissaries of my existence, they burst in rapid succession on the surface of the water as if announcing my location to the breathing world.

I shuddered like a spirit trapped in a corpse. That's when I knew that as much as I feared death, I hated it perhaps even more. Death was an enemy, a curse to me, something never meant to be by all that is holy. I would do everything in my power to resist its reach. Better to live in fear of it. Better to die fighting in Vietnam—in the end a soldier simply fights for his life. Better to accept the challenges of living than to lie down for the frigid silence of death's ultimate insult. The bottom of the Columbia would be the tomb of nothing more than my hesitation. With that, I kicked for the world above.

"Whew!" I screamed, breaking the surface. "Yes! Yes!

Yes!" my laughter echoed back to me like applause from the sheer walls along the river. Treading water, I looked up at the empty cliff top, wishing Gordon were there. I could hear him calling, *"Do it, you nit!"*

Of all people, he deserved to see this passage in my life. I could only imagine the trials he and his buddies were facing on the battlefields of Southeast Asia. Their daily struggles made my small dive into reality seem petty and insignificant.

Rightfully so, I thought as I breaststroked toward the cliff. Taking hold of a gray-black stone at the base of a steep chimney, I overrode my natural acrophobia and scaled it. Reaching the top, I pushed myself through the plunge again, for no one else but me.

BECOMING MEN

Born opposites, Gordon and I continued to make decisions as we left home that drove us along separate paths. After graduation I decided to attend a Bible college in California instead of the local community college he had attended.

I selected college in about the same way I had purchased the motorcycle. It was not a decision reached through careful deliberation. Rather, I bounced like a pinball according to a growing sense of desperation.

Looking back on it, the choice was primarily driven by a fear of going to war and a desperate need to control that violent part of myself I had discovered after the beating by the bully. These two fears had become closely linked in my mind, and they fed one another like gasoline to an open flame.

Seeing that relationship between the two fears, however, did nothing to set me free of their tyranny.

To my way of thinking back then, Gordon had gone to Vietnam because he did not suffer my level of fear. He could act like a true soldier because he had confidence in himself. I felt sure that, just as he had stood up to the bully, he showed true courage in the face of the Viet Cong. I, on the other hand, would risk either cowardice or an insane rage that might endanger everything and everyone around me.

Military service seemed like a suicide mission for me. Studying Bible and theology, then, was a way to throw myself in the opposite direction of uncontrolled violence and the cowardice that drove me to it. In Bible college, I would receive a ministerial student deferment from the draft; plus, I would not be likely to encounter more bullies.

In taking this direction, I drew also from Griz's example. He had been that brawling, boozing lumberjack before becoming a preacher. His dark side had disappeared into the ministry; Gordon and I had both seen the very real elements of his new life. Even on hunting and fishing trips, Griz would praise God aloud for the wonders of creation. He would read from Scripture around the campfire, and pray a blessing over simple lunch-meat sandwiches. Gordon had found little value in all of that, but I still couldn't adequately define my life apart from it. In this way, too, my choice to attend Bible college was an attempt to propel myself in the safe and familiar direction Griz had chosen.

There were other elements behind the decision, also. I wanted to prepare for the ministry because a very real part of me simply wanted to follow God. Griz had led both

Gordon and me in the childhood prayer, "God be merciful to me a sinner." For me, the prayer had always seemed genuine. To my mind, I had received the kingdom of God into myself as a five-year-old, repeating the words in simple faith. With that formula, I sensed that I had received eternal life as a divine gift—something I now had to carefully maintain or I would certainly lose it. I sensed divine eyes watching me, even in private times, and I felt accountable. As the years had passed, I imagined myself in a nearly constant conversation with the Lord. From moment to moment I would seek His forgiveness from sinful thoughts and actions.

This spiritual state produced both fear and comfort in me, depending upon my performance of the Christian life. Most of the time, true to my nature, it produced fear. When doing bad, I feared I might lose my soul. When doing good, I thought I deserved heaven—which was not often. With this history of spiritual fear, as I left home, I sensed more than ever a nagging need to score points with God. Going to Bible college seemed like something that would do that in spades.

Finally, among my reasons for going, Griz had wanted nothing more than to have a son follow him in ministry. I wanted to be that son, to please him, and to finally beat Gordon at something. One day I lumped all of these confused reasons under the simple statement, "Dad, I feel called to preach," and Griz took it at face value.

He became enthusiastic and suggested a school in Seattle, an institution governed by his denominational district. Though I wanted to follow in his footsteps, I didn't want to walk that close. So I chose the denomination's sister school near San Francisco. An independent choice, yet not too independent.

Gordon served a second term in Vietnam as the war escalated. That same year found me safe from the draft, a freshman, majoring in Bible and theology in California. I relished the study, yet my unresolved conflicts moved me toward the image of "campus radical." I bought a '64 Volkswagen beetle, and on weekends traveled to San Francisco's Haight-Ashbury district, a personal curiosity that grew into something of an ongoing investigation.

It was the year of wearing flowers in the hair. Everywhere across the nation, members of my generation were growing shaggy, donning headbands and Bohemian beads, flashing peace signs, dropping out, hitchhiking, listening to rock music, and living a new morality—much like the old immorality. I enjoyed the music but didn't understand the rest of it one bit.

Every trip to Haight-Ashbury became a private quest to answer the question, What in the world is going on here? My closest brush with hippie enlightenment came through the words of a tie-dyed druggie resembling a young Dennis Hopper; he looked at me through red-rimmed eyes and mused, "You don't know what's happenin', man?" Then he chuckled imperiously, "Man, it's happenin' without you." I couldn't have agreed more. I seemed lost to my own generation.

In an effort to get "in touch," I expanded my horizons

in the musical direction. Rediscovering my buried feelings for that mandolin, I took voice lessons and auditioned and won a place in the college choir, singing bass. After a year, I had not only joined all of the school's musical performance groups, but I broke the school's behavioral tradition by forming a jazz-rock ensemble with twelve Bay Area musicians. We called ourselves the Brotherhood, and we began to perform in northern California.

Gordon and I had no direct communication during this time. The first contact between us other than secondhand reports came during my second year of college, shortly after his discharge. I worried about his homecoming. On Berkeley, San Francisco, and San Jose State University campuses, I had seen Vietnam vets jeered. Nixon's policy of *Vietnamization*, the process of replacing American troops with Vietnamese soldiers, had produced a sudden and unexpected impatience back home. Even Middle Americans were beginning to demand an immediate end to the war. I felt sure that Gordon would receive no hero's welcome under this growing political cloud. No marching bands, no public speeches or appearances, no proud newspaper mention, no commendations for his war wounds. At least our family could count its blessings. Unlike other friends whose young men were eventually listed on that black slab in Washington, D.C., we could thank God for his safe return. I telephoned to welcome him home.

"Stay in that preacher school, Steve," he warned somberly. "Don't let 'em draft you. Believe me, Nam's not worth one wasted minute of your life."

I felt a strange loss in these words. The Gordon I had

known, the gung ho soldier who had leaped from the cliff, seemed to have gone over the hill with "Abraham, Martin, and John." He had once overcome fear, heroically. Even the fear of death. He had demonstrated superior willpower to me and had shown a soldier's courage to fight and kill. Now, he called it a waste. Even though I had not been able to live up to his standard, I had wanted to. Maybe next year, I thought; maybe someday I would rise above myself and reach his level. But what would it mean if he had abandoned his ideals and his place as a role model? It would mean no more than reciting shooting statistics alone over a plate of venison.

I recall the heat of emotion building in my face as I walked a path through the California redwoods, contemplating the meaning of his words. He had not only claimed that his choice to go to Vietnam had been wrong, but he seemed to be saying that I had chosen well by going to Bible college.

I knew better than that. My decision had been made out of sheer desperation, not wisdom. How could Gordon look up to me? Even more, how could I let him? The dilemma seemed reminiscent of the time he had bragged about me riding the worn-out bull. Once again, I let a false impression stand uncorrected, and now I felt as counterfeit as a two-fingered peace sign.

After his discharge, Gordon took a job on a registered Hereford cattle ranch near Portland. He bought a new Firebird and soon announced that he would marry Cheryl, a hometown girl four years his junior. I remembered Cheryl from high school but hoped that she would not remember me. She had been among those watching the infamous fist fight.

Gordon, hearing of my new musical interests at college, asked me to sing a solo at their wedding. He was most pleased to hear about my jazz-rock ensemble; apparently I had failed to mention that, as a bass vocalist, I merely sang backup. I flew home for the occasion. The song they had selected didn't fit my voice range, but I altered the key and sang it anyway. I recall rendering it badly, feeling embarrassed. My arms actually began to feel numb during the performance, and my fingertips tingled. The truth is, I feared I might faint before finishing. The Oregon boy who could perform with confidence before strangers, choked trying to impress 'em back home.

I shared the experience with my voice teacher when I returned to school. He looked at me strangely and said, "Man, you really get uptight." After a thoughtful pause he said, "Why did this song have so much to do with you anyway? Who were you singing for? Yourself?"

The truth kicked like a rifle. Stung by his observation, I couldn't answer. I realized that my stage fright, simply another form of fear, had plagued me because I stood in the center of my own little universe. For the first time I saw how *selfish* fear was. Unfortunately, gaining this insight did nothing to set me on the right path. *How could a person get beyond himself?* I wondered. I hadn't a clue.

A week after the wedding, Gordon and Cheryl surprised me by dropping by my room at college. They had secretly targeted the romantic Monterey Peninsula for their honeymoon. Our short half day together was pleasant, but it surprised me how proud Gordon seemed to be of me for forming the jazz-rock band. In truth I had the least talent of any member of the group. They were the true musicians, recognized for their skill. I couldn't read a note of music. I was merely the visionary dervish who drove them in the wrong artistic direction as often as the right one. They were constantly cleaning up my inspirational messes. Yet, for that evening with Gordon and Cheryl, I performed well; we went to a Santa Cruz restaurant and enjoyed talk of irrelevant matters until they made their way south.

As I began my junior year, my campus radical image became superheated. Unable to contain my insecurities any longer, I protested and attacked institutional hypocrisy wherever I found it. Primarily, I resisted the school dress code because it had been used to exclude hippies from campus. I had found the immature man's best friend: a self-righteous cause.

If I had demanded of myself the same standards that I suddenly began to demand of school policy, I would have found some common ground with them. I might have remained reasonable in my criticisms. We might have negotiated and made progress. But I didn't do that. I used the Bible knowledge they had given me to provoke and challenge them ruthlessly. Growing my hair long and dressing in surplus military fatigues, I violated the dress code and threw in my lot with the hippie outcasts. Then I published my protest in the school paper in a poem titled "My First Day on the Cross," identifying my social crusade with the cause of Jesus Christ.

Fearing the numbers of impressionable students I might lead astray, school administrators made an example of me and kicked me out. Furthermore, they added an unprecedented ruling that I would not be allowed to return, even if I repented. Their reasons? I had not just disagreed with school authority; I had defied it. In open forum I had stated my case from Scripture so adamantly that the administration had been embarrassed while the student body had overwhelmingly backed me. Adding to my rebellious profile, an administrator privately told me, the jazz-rock band I had founded had raised serious concerns among the school's substantial California donors.

A semester later the school altered its dress code, as I had suggested, but still they would not allow me to return to enjoy it. "Find some place where you can fit in," the admissions officer said. "Don't go to a private Bible college, please. Spare them, and spare yourself. You don't belong. Maybe you should try a state school where they seem to value your kind of dissent."

So much for my desire to follow Griz in the pulpit. This rejection really hurt. Deep down, in spite of my defiance, I wanted the school to care enough to set me straight, not set me free.

The worst blow came a short time later when my jazz-rock group asked me to depart for pushing an obscure musical agenda called "apocalyptic rock." I seemed to be on a roll—downhill. As for apocalyptic rock, the musicians felt that end-of-the-world concepts did not lend themselves to good music. To my ear, the clashing sounds of apocalypse made perfect sense. My world, if not ending, was certainly falling apart. And looking around at the discordant way America seemed to be tearing itself asunder, the idea seemed ripe for a popular audience as well. Yet, unable to sell my musical vision, I had grown shrill and uncompromising. They had finally had enough.

While still absorbing this loss, I learned that Gordon had been fired from the registered Hereford cattle ranch near Portland, where he had worked since getting married. He had been so proud of the job, I mused. Surely he was not going through the same kind of tailspin?

When I called for his explanation, he claimed that the ranch had turned out not to be worth his time. It existed, he said, so that a bunch of rich city owners could write off taxes and expenses. Even though he and Cheryl were now the proud parents of a baby daughter, he would simply not lie down for that kind of operation—voicing an attitude with an uncomfortably familiar ring to me.

Then, I thought that perhaps his decision to leave the ranch, unlike my own expulsion, had been made on sound principle. This possibility seemed plausible because he had already taken another offer as foreman on a "real working ranch" back home, near Pendleton. He at least had not been dumped into thin air, as I had been. He had found a place to take care of his growing family and his ranching ambition at the same time. In closing our conversation, he mentioned that, by the way, he had traded his Firebird for a new Corvette Stingray. I was impressed.

Reluctantly, I told him I had been kicked out of the "preacher school," which meant that I had lost my draft deferment. I asked him what he thought I should do about it.

"What's your number?"

"110."

"You're dead meat," he said. "Look, you can't let them take you over there. I served two terms in Nam. That's enough for both of us."

"I appreciate that, brother, but I don't think the government will buy it."

"That's why you will have to get yourself back here and argue a conscientious objector status with the home draft board—or else head for Canada. That's all the choice you've got."

"I won't go to Canada," I said immediately. It wasn't merely patriotism on my part, but the very mention of Canada made me feel cold, wet, and alone. I already felt alienated enough.

"Well," he continued, "this is a redneck draft board up here, brother. These are cowboys, farmers, and ranchers, so you better come up with a mighty good argument."

"I will," I promised.

Strangely, I looked forward to petitioning the draft board. Though I had failed to win my arguments at Bible college and with the Brotherhood, I had an instinct that told me I would win this one. When I examined my feelings, I realized that part of the reason for my confidence lay in the serious way I had studied Scripture at school. I knew Bible and theology pretty well. This had worked against me at college because I had used it to shame the authorities, but I believed the same diligence would impress the draft board. They would not feel threatened or competitive over the finer points I brought to the argument. In all likelihood, this rural Oregon board had not dealt with many draftees who were skilled in quoting Scripture anyway.

Furthermore, if I had accurately sensed the impatience of Middle America as a result of *Vietnamization*, then it followed that draft boards would now want to keep every young man out of the war they possibly could. I would merely have to give them a legitimate case. In that mix of reasons I gained an unusual confidence.

Immediately, my new focus shifted from music to honing an argument for the draft board. I used the book of Romans, chapter 13 to prepare my defense, the very passage many people used to justify placing Christians in military service. I liked the defiant element in my unorthodox style. No conservative biblical scholar would respect my arguments; so much the better. I would win without their approval. None of my Bible professors would salute my hermeneutics; fine. They were hypocrites anyway. As the coup de grâce in my crusade, I had carved out a position my own father opposed; all the better. After a lifetime of keeping my opinions to myself, I would now unleash them, independent of Griz.

Let the chips fall where they may, I thought. If I win, I win alone. If I lose—? Well, I made no plans for that. I packed the Volkswagen and headed for Oregon to make those arguments before Local Board Number Twenty-Five.

Arriving there, I discovered that Gordon had been fired from the "real working ranch." This was unsettling news.

I asked him what had gone wrong, and he explained that he had gotten into a fight with the ranch owner, who had naturally sent him packing. Gordon didn't blame him, he said; he just disagreed with him. His also explained that his Corvette Stingray had been totaled in an accident. He now drove a beat-up pickup, lived in a dingy Pendleton apartment, and had been forced to use food stamps to feed his family. Furthermore, he now worked night shift at a mental hospital, on the wing for the severely retarded.

I could not imagine this. How could my independent cowboy brother possibly be on welfare? Even harder to imagine—how could he fit in the environs of a mental hospital?

"This is the kind of Alternate Service you will have to do if you become a conscientious objector," Gordon warned. "You'll have to do two years in community work. Might as well come spend a night shift with me and see what this job is like. You might like it."

Weeks later, following my appearance and delivery of written arguments before the draft board and while I still awaited their verdict, Gordon secured a pass for me to spend the night with him at the mental hospital. The sights, smells, and sounds of that ward seemed to validate every panic attack I had ever known. Amid a cacophony of moans, screeches, laughter, crying, and unintelligible eruptions, these malformed human beings, some as grotesque as the Elephant Man, existed in a shunned world I had never imagined so close to home. More than a hundred on Gordon's ward lurched about like lost souls, gesturing and chattering incessantly. Seldom interacting, they strolled or lay alone on cots, each abandoned to his own mind.

The thing that struck the most fear in my heart was to know that these zombies were human beings, like me. In the first few seconds of being there, I knew that, like Vietnam, I would never follow my brother here. The scene would drive me crazy. Unable to tell Gordon my true thoughts, I became similar to the lobotomized beasts around me, wandering through the night shift in a haze of my own unspoken fears.

By contrast, Gordon seemed to have his emotions and thoughts well in hand. His approach seemed not only practical, but oddly informed. He knew most patients by name and a good deal about their families. He also knew the names of their disorders, disabilities, and medications.

He took me on a tour of the floor, introducing me to savants, autistics, and mentally retarded patients. For each he had a greeting, whether or not they could respond. It reminded me of the competent way he had treated cattle and horses. I recalled that he had always enjoyed the veterinary aspects of working stock—administering shots, binding wounds, applying liniment, pulling calves with forceps. Here he seemed to apply the same abilities, only now he herded people—who behaved oddly like cattle— and administered prescribed pills by the cupload.

"Medicine," he said as he measured out dosages, "has made straightjackets and solitary confinement obsolete."

He took me on a tour of the shower rooms to show me where these pitiful creatures had been washed with hoses earlier in the evening. The smell of feces and urine lingered faintly in the air. As Gordon removed a high pressure disinfectant hose from the wall, he pointed to an "excrement eater" who had stolen into the shower room, looking for the object of his appetite.

"I told you to stay out of here," he scolded.

As the guilty party slunk away, Gordon turned to me with a wink. "He'll be back."

He opened the hose nozzle and washed the room down again for good measure. I swallowed my revulsion, nearly fainting. As we exited, I detected a perverse smile at the corners of Gordon's mouth. He never ceased to enjoy tweaking my sensitivities.

He next took me to visit the bed of his favorite patient, a savant who could recite the names and terms of office of nearly every political officer in the state of Oregon. The man suffered also from a disorder that left him frozen in a fetal position. Gordon spoke to him with affection and pride. He bragged on him, telling me that the patient had come from a prominent family in Oregon politics. "You would recognize their name if I told you," he said. "But that information's classified."

He lifted the man's curled body in his arms and carried him to a toilet, strapping him to it. He stood back and announced proudly that this patient never dirtied his bed.

"Yeah, yeah," the man agreed, looking up at Gordon sideways, the only angle at which he could turn his head.

Gordon explained to me that he had made it his personal mission to see that the patient never had to lie in discomfort in his bed waiting to go to the toilet. "If he has the dignity to hold it, I'm not going to have him in pain," Gordon declared.

The pitiful man added noises of his approval.

Next, Gordon carried him around the ward so that he could engage in a ritual of conversations with a few of the less retarded patients. Then he returned him to bed, tucked him in, and bid him good night.

As night grew into early morning, I asked Gordon how he had learned so many details about the patients.

"Follow me," he said.

We walked to the central part of the ward and entered a glass cubicle. From inside, we could view the expanse of the ward in all directions. We each took a seat on a tall stool. Gordon shook a Marlboro from his pack, lighting it up. Then he reached into a corner behind him and pulled out a worn acoustical guitar. I waited curiously for him to answer my question. He seemed to ignore it.

"I learned to play some in Vietnam," he said, strumming a sequence of carefully studied chords. "Bought this Martin ripoff in Hong Kong on R and R." He strummed another chord, then broke into a finger-picked melody. "These patients like music," he said, looking up at me. "Soothes the savage beast." His eyes sparkled at me above the smoldering cigarette in his mouth.

He suddenly put the guitar down and reached over to a large horizontal filing drawer, opening it. The system of drawers nearly circled the entire cubicle at waist level. He gestured for me to have a look. "This stuff is classified, but you can have a peek. It's here, if you want to work here."

I removed a file about an inch thick and opened it. The volume of medical information under the name of this particular patient seemed mind boggling. "This is how you learned about these guys?"

Gordon scooted back onto the stool. "I'm here all night. What am I gonna do?"

I looked back at the file in my hand, then at the number of file drawers around me, realizing the amount of study he had put into his short time here. Then I looked out at the dim ward. A few of the hyperactive patients still wandered around. Most shifted beneath their blankets under the dimmed lights.

. . . *I would not have done what Gordon has done here,* I thought. *I just want out.*

He looked up, glancing around the quiet ward. Then he turned with a sly grin; "Gil and Rowdy, that's us."

The names rang a bell for me, a faint one. "Gil Favor," I said aloud. I recalled the one rare week night in the late '60s when Griz, Gordon, and I could be found watching "Rawhide," a black-and-white TV western series. The show built its weekly episodes around cattle drives. The main characters were the trail boss Gil Favor and his brooding sidekick Rowdy Yates.

"Gil and Rowdy," Gordon repeated lightly as he began to pick out the show's familiar theme song. Suddenly and spontaneously, we bellowed "Raw-*hide!*"

Several patients shot erect on their beds, looking for the culprits who had distrubed their peace. We laughed perhaps a bit too hard. Heaven knows we needed to ease some tension. Intending no disrespect for the pitiful creatures on the ward, we just required a break after spending several hours cooped up with a hundred genetic tragedies.

Gordon went on playing more soothing melodies, and we sang quietly, spinning a cushion of sanity around ourselves. *He must have learned to do this in Vietnam,* I thought somberly. I watched his fingers work the Martin rip-off with growing respect, sensing a new gulf between us. Until now, we had been separated by fear, courage, and willpower—this time, surprisingly, it was by compassion. Gordon, for all of his cowboy toughness, had found a way to continue caring for these extremely difficult people in the mental hospital. By contrast, I had not been able to overcome my own assaulted feelings long enough to make myself useful.

Days later, the draft board summoned me to appear for their verdict. A spokeswoman for the group told me that they had unanimously granted the conscientious objector status I had sought. Taking extra time to express her admiration for my knowledge of the Bible and my deep personal commitment to live by its principles, she went on to say that they were proud to award Alternate Service to one who would take such moral convictions into the arena of community service.

Recalling Gordon's compassion at the mental hospital and my lack thereof, I tried to ignore the hypocrisy in accepting this compliment. In conclusion, the board spokeswoman said that they had seen a lot of phony draft dodgers in their time, but were glad to have found the real thing at last.

Later, Gordon added his stamp of approval. "Nam's a cruel joke. I'm nothin' but proud of you, brother."

From this comment, apparently he saw my approach as a ploy to avoid Vietnam and nothing more. But to the best of my knowledge, it was more than that to me. Not wanting to believe or accept his limited view, I reminded myself that I had passionately believed every argument I had made to the board. Still, Gordon's backhanded compliment made me feel uncomfortable about it.

"Well, do you want to do your Alternate Service at the hospital?" he asked. "I can pull a few strings."

"No, thanks. I, uh—I have several opportunities back in California. I'll leave the hospital here in your good hands."

My stint with Alternate Service began with an entry level job at Goodwill's processing plant in Santa Cruz, California. I began as a textile worker in their sheltered rehabilitation workshop. Perhaps I had found my true level of competence at last; practically no responsibility went with the assignment. I merely had been hired to fill an empty slot among the handicapped workers and a cluster of unemployable felons.

Not one to let reality inhibit me, on the paltry sum of $1.65 per hour, in December I married an eighteen-year-old California wine country beauty. Her traditional parents would have nothing to do with our union, but in the heat of youthful rebellion, we drove off in my Volkswagen, wearing their rejection like a badge of honor. They, in turn, boycotted the wedding and reception.

For a few months afterward, it looked as though we might ride our rebellious magic carpet skyward against the odds. Later in December, I was invited to perform as a soloist in the San Francisco Sacred Concert Society's annual Christmas concert. The following February, I auditioned for a holiday television musical under production in the Bay Area and unexpectedly won the leading role. Soloist, television actor—suddenly, to our naive eyes, my hapless Goodwill career looked like a launching pad to stardom.

Meanwhile, I learned that Gordon had left his job at the mental hospital. I called for an explanation and got the story from Cheryl; it seems Gordon was riding fence on the high plains at the time. She said that he had been offered the foremanship on one of the most picturesque spreads in eastern Oregon and had gladly traded in his service on the mental ward. I did not probe to find out what had happened to his humanitarian commitment to the retarded patients because it eased my personal guilt just to know that he had quit. Beyond that, I also wanted to believe that we were both finally getting our lives on the proper track.

But Gordon was soon fired again, and then again. In the months to follow it became almost impossible to keep track of him. He couldn't seem to avoid battles with his bosses. Then I learned that he had enrolled in a local college in LaGrande, Oregon, majoring in geology. On the side, he did odd jobs and participated in a politically radical theater company. Meanwhile, Cheryl became pregnant—and then, bang-bang—twice more, delivering sons into the family.

My upward mobility was also short-lived. I sang two years running in the Christmas concert, but by late that first spring, the TV production company had run out of money. My dreams of stardom vanished as quickly as they had arisen. Perhaps the best thing about this flirtation with the performing arts was the look it gave me at the work behind the scenes. Writing, directing, and producing fascinated me far more than acting or singing. I began to carry a pencil and pad at my Goodwill work station, trying my hand as a beginning playwright.

After three months of married life, renting a $90-per-month studio apartment near the Santa Cruz beach, my wife announced that she was pregnant. By no means did I feel ready for the approach of fatherhood, not to mention ready for any of the other challenges multiplying around me. Instead of dealing with it, I buried myself in work.

Within one month I was promoted to department head, which raised my pay to $2.65 per hour. Two months later, another promotion to division head brought my salary to nearly $5 per hour. As a mere twenty-two-year-old, I became responsible for fifty employees. At this moment of opportunity, I butted heads with the plant's executive director. Perhaps, like Gordon, I simply felt compelled to battle anyone in authority. At any rate, I received a memo on the morning of June 23, 1972: "Your termination check will be ready for you to pick up at the bookkeeping office today." My wife was now three months pregnant. Hello, unemployment line.

In December, my wife gave birth to a beautiful son. In January, as America signed the Paris cease-fire, I left my music experimentation behind in the San Francisco area and moved my family to Phoenix, Arizona, where I sought to enter the world of behind-the-scenes TV production. I took a studio job at a nonprofit broadcasting station, which provided Arizona's Spanish-speaking population its only television source. But after three months, as I sought to qualify the job with my draft board, the station manager wrote me a short letter: "We have appreciated your work here and your contribution. You will find your check enclosed." The reference to my "contribution" seemed generous; a few days earlier I had accidentally broadcast a Roadrunner cartoon soundtrack over a live Spanish newscast.

Adding to my difficulties, Alternate Service positions had become scarce in the early '70s. No longer fantasizing about a military victory in Vietnam, draft boards had found new and "honorable" ways to keep young men from fleeing to Canada. Primarily, they loosened the rules under which they would grant conscientious objector status, and many young men were finding that loophole. The ranks of conscientious objectors swelled with a flood of new pacifists.

As I sought to find a final Alternate Service position, the war in Vietnam ended. By April of '73 the last American troops were home. Even so, as a conscientious objector I owed my country another year of my life.

In midsummer I finally landed an assignment at a depressing little program for supposedly nonviolent youth offenders in Arizona's Sonoran Desert. Upon my arrival in the 115-degree heat of August, the draft board sent a letter of welcome and warning to me: "If you knowingly fail or neglect to perform satisfactorily this assigned Alternate Service you may be referred for prosecution." They also sent a letter to the program's director: "We ask that you notify this office immediately should this employee be terminated sooner than July 11, 1974, his expiration date." Apparently the draft board would not stand for my being fired again.

The new program seemed totally uninspired. Until my release, my duties would involve spending nights with fifty-five testosterone-driven young men who had already outsmarted authorities enough to have been removed from decent society. The program's limited facilities totalled three dormitories—supervised nightly by myself and two co-workers—a crude dining hall, a basketball court, and a makeshift softball diamond. Our main tools for control were behavior score charts—we carried our ever present clipboards—and the threat of lock-up, or "shipping out." The facility was a last stop before prison for many of these malcontents—and now, in light of the draft board warning, perhaps for me, too.

While learning the ropes at the new program I gravitated toward an experienced Hispanic coworker named Sanchez. He seemed idolized among the population and I could see why; he was handsome, friendly, and wore sports jerseys that allowed him to display his abundance of bulging muscles. An Arizona State University wrestling team member, he kept his long black hair tucked constantly in a red headband. His very presence made me feel backed up in this threatening place, the way I had felt when Gordon had been an upperclassman back in high school.

During the evening hours I helped Sanchez supervise softball, basketball, football, boxing, and other sports activities. It was our hope to exhaust the energy level of our charges before darkness fell. After they had been successfully put to bed I would search him out for tips on dealing with the various personalities and supervising problems I encountered.

A few weeks into the assignment I received an indication of how very tricky this program might be. One night, a smaller boy known to the others as a "snitch," gave information leading Sanchez and me to a large cache of paint cans used for fume sniffing—also known as "huffing"—a brain-damaging way to get high. The snitch pled with us to protect him as we incinerated the lot in a steel barrel. As far as we knew, we had done everything necessary to protect his identity; it turned out we had underestimated the criminal grapevine.

Suddenly, a sizable sixteen-year-old from Sanchez's dormitory snatched a softball bat and headed for the third coworker's residence, where the snitch lived. He promised loudly to "bash his head in" for ratting.

I naturally waited for Sanchez to take charge, but he seemed flustered and indecisive. As I watched him, my jaw dropped. I simply could not believe that the most macho figure among us seemed as paralyzed as I had been as a boy. Meanwhile, real violence threatened.

Something inside of me snapped. I found myself running after the culprit, hearing my voice boom that he would deeply regret it if he didn't drop the weapon at once. He ignored me and kept on course. Meanwhile, all fifty-plus hoodlums surrounded me with a wall of glee, taunting, ridiculing, and promising graphically that I would be the one to regret interfering.

I had no plan, absolutely no idea what I would do; I only knew that the guy with the bat was the one in real danger. All the red-eyed rage I had felt for the Oregon bully was back. Under these special circumstances, I no longer felt fear.

As I approached the sixteen-year-old from the back side, he turned and swung the bat—but I was already in his face. The weapon passed behind me, into the dust. Meanwhile, I had taken two fistfuls of his fashionably long hair and, with great force, bent him backward to the ground. He screamed with rage, but I told him, with even more rage, to shut up. Without striking the boy, I forced him to lay in the dirt until I gave him permission to rise. After testing me twice more, and receiving the same humiliation, he agreed to obey.

Suddenly, I was up again, snatching up the bat. I walked around the circle of thugs, holding it out, promising that if they took a weapon or engaged in any act of violence on my watch, they would proceed "over my dead body."

By now, their former taunts had turned into a few reasonable requests that I show the kid in the dirt some mercy. Apparently, much more than I knew, I had taken charge of the situation.

When all had finally quieted down and the population was in bed I found Sanchez in the kitchen. I asked him why he hadn't stepped into the crisis himself. To my amazement, he looked at me and shook his head with admiration. "I don't know how to do what you did, man," he said. "You were in a total rage, but you were in control. I'm afraid that if he had swung that bat at me I would have killed him, or at least I would have beaten him too severely and I'd be the one going to jail. Once I get started in something like that, I don't know when to stop. You do."

I didn't know anything of the kind. I puzzled long over his words and never did make sense of them. It had never been about starting or stopping. The whole incident had been about taking responsibility for the smaller boy in our care.

From then on, Sanchez came to me for advice and help with his problems. I found this disturbing. All my life I had been programmed by Gordon's voice calling me a "crybaby," a "tattletale baby," a "girl." And in more recent years I had seemed to be the "yellow-bellied coward" and "wimpy preacher's kid" the Oregon bully had called me. Suddenly, unexpectedly, I had forged a new identity for myself in Arizona. It took months to absorb it as being real.

The morning after the incident the boys started calling me "the enforcer." There were affection and admiration in their eyes. I quickly learned that for all of their threatening ways, these social rejects were terrified and would submit to someone they perceived to be stronger. My strength had not come from bulging biceps, or even from willpower, but from caring enough to put myself on the line.

More violent situations tested my resolve in the months ahead. While on an outing with a dozen boys in the Superstition Wilderness, an otherwise charming young man disappeared ahead of the pack, only to roll a boulder from a cliff more than one hundred feet directly above us. I hunted him down and hauled him to jail, only to find out later that he had poisoned his own father before coming to our program. He should never have been admitted.

On another occasion I disarmed a boy attacking another with a bowie knife. Again, I disarmed an offender brandishing a set of horseshoes. One night the entire population rioted, cutting power to the facilities and taking hostages. By starlight, I negotiated a resolution, using my Volkswagen to drive the wounded to the hospital and the guilty to jail. In lockup a few days later, three of my charges lured a guard to the bars of their cell and strangled him to death.

At this point I began to realize that something was seriously wrong with this Alternate Service assignment. Truly violent offenders were being lumped together with kids who merely needed guidance.

My final violent confrontation resulted in injury. While disarming a boy with a pair of scissors I received a gash on the forehead. That night, lying in the hospital receiving eight stitches, I took stock of myself. I realized that I might have called the police in some of these situations if I had not felt the need to exorcise my own demon of cowardice. Because of that need I had enjoyed playing the enforcer. But now, that part of the issue was behind me. Sooner or later, if I kept playing that role, I would actually assist in bringing real harm to the boys I sought to protect.

One month before my release from Alternate Service, I faced another threat of violence. Instead of handling the situation alone, I called the police. The resulting firestorm of state examination blew the lid off the real problem with the program. It appeared that these seriously impaired offenders sprinkled throughout the population had been accepted so the program could receive the state funding that went with them. Mammon ruled.

At this point, the program director found reason to fire me. I knew that if he also contacted my draft board, I would soon find myself in court, and possibly in jail. I immediately appealed to the board of directors. As a result of their hearing, within two weeks I was reinstated, and the boss who had fired me went down the road looking for another job. One month later I successfully completed my obligation of service to my country, and I could sense my life beginning to turn around.

Rather than leave the program, I opted to stay and see the changes implemented. I also decided to take full advantage of the night shift by enrolling as a student at Arizona State University in Tempe. Losing a full year of credits in the transfer from the California school, I nevertheless targeted an English degree, which, upon completion, would send me in the direction of a writing career.

For the next two years, I began to put my life on a more productive track. In the process, I experienced a spiritual awakening. Brought low by my record of failures, I began to pray with more depth of meaning, looking beyond my own ambitions for the higher purposes of God in life. I began to attend church with a deeper sense of appreciation. My relationship to God moved from needing to score points to wanting to serve out of gratitude. At the university, I discovered a Catholic professor of English literature, a man of profound faith. His courses on Milton's *Paradise Lost* and Biblical Backgrounds to English Literature enriched the historical and intellectual dimensions of my faith.

But during these very busy years of my life, working full-time and going to school, I had little contact with my family. I heard nothing from my brother Gordon: no letters, no phone calls. In the meantime, Griz had moved the rest of the family to Alaska. He now could preach and hunt moose, not to mention fish those unequalled waters of the last frontier.

In 1976 I graduated from ASU with a degree in English. After several months of job hunting, I found a beginning writing position with a North Carolina television production company. Moving to the East Coast with my wife and four-year-old son, I began working long hours to make up for the lost time in my career. My two brief exposures to the TV business seemed to have stood me in good stead. My new supervisors often praised my work. I let them think whatever they wanted to think. In truth, this job was all "earn while you learn," for me.

Within months, I found opportunities to direct some of my own commercial scripts, using local actors and an occasional celebrity spokesperson. Soon afterward, the responsibility of producing came my way. Commercials and documentary productions bearing my credits began to be exhibited nationwide. Some were noticed back home, to my pleasure.

To Griz and the family in Alaska, this new level of achievement in my life seemed to have come out of the blue. Through letters and phone calls, I tried to let them know of the many changes that had been made during the hard times in Arizona. I had hit bottom and had rebounded with a whole new set of priorities that guided me in better directions now.

Meanwhile, Gordon's reputation slipped in the opposite direction. It seemed that he had run out of ranches to work in eastern Oregon, gaining a reputation for being highly talented but "unmanageable." Even in Alaska, the family heard rumors that he associated with a new cadre of Oregon friends who participated in illegal commerce. Drugs and gunrunning were part of the picture. He had grown his hair long and had covered his handsome face with a thick growth of beard.

All this talk filtered my way via telephone conversations couched in the hushed tones of mystery. Who was Gordon after all? Had Vietnam changed him? Why couldn't the family's number-one son succeed like his younger brother? Had anyone ever really known him?

I began to feel that, in fact, I *did* know Gordon. Perhaps we had been much more alike than either of us had suspected. His personal tailspin made sense as I looked back and compared it to my own. The instability could be explained, not by willpower, but by *fear*-power. The more I pondered it, the more I could see that Gordon and I had been driven by the same insane fears; we had simply chosen different paths in dealing with them. I also knew that as I had begun to deal more successfully with fear, so could he.

Griz and I communicated only occasionally about Gordon during this time. At one point he confided to me in a tone of regret and sadness that Gordon no longer made any attempt to "live for God," as he put it.

"I think Vietnam has done a number on Gordon," he said. "You know, he was in the middle of the worst fighting over there. It was not like World War II; we had the country's support back then. He comes back here to all this

Mai Lai Massacre stuff, talk of 'fragging,' and Watergate. You can't blame some of these young guys for losing faith in the normal course of justice. Still, 'every tub's gotta stand on its own bottom.' A guy who blames everything on everyone else soon learns to justify his own hypocrisy, even criminal activity."

Hearing this, I could not help but wonder what would have happened to me if I had served over there. To a certain degree, Gordon had taken my place. I wanted to do something now to help him, if I could.

One winter day, a couple of dark-suited men appeared at Griz's office in Alaska. Once inside, they flashed badges, informing him that they were FBI operatives working a case in the Pacific Northwest, specifically in eastern Oregon, where he had once lived with his family. As they asked a battery of questions about Gordon and his circle of friends, Griz realized that his son was headed for serious trouble. In fact, he suspected that the detectives had come to warn him as much as to get information. From their remarks, they seemed to hold Gordon in higher regard than the others in his circle, and they wished aloud that he would do better for himself.

Griz paid Gordon a visit. He told me later that he counselled Gordon straight-up about changing his ways but remained skeptical that anything permanent would result. "Talk is cheap," he concluded. "It's like I told him, 'Only getting right with God will do the real job.'"

Dad's a preacher, I thought; *always will be.* He only knows one kind of change—a catastrophic, spiritual about-face—the kind he experienced in that tent revival so long

ago. I didn't knock it, but I had experienced another kind
of change in recent years that had come slowly and painfully, like untangling a bad knot. It had been accomplished
through a relentless series of hard times. My adult spiritual
awakening had not arrived out of the blue, but had been
bound up with the other complicated needs inside of me.
When they were set right, the spiritual aspect seemed to
come along with it.

Gordon, I thought, must have the same spirituality
inside him that I had. It had been likewise tangled up with
a lot of desperate drives and inner fears. I hoped that,
perhaps, through my Arizona years, I had discovered keys
that Gordon might put to some good use.

One early spring day in 1977 my employer unexpectedly
asked me to fly to Seattle on urgent business. Something
clicked in my mind. I sensed that God had engineered this
circumstance so that I could get back together with my
brother. Before I left my boss's office that day, I had cashed
in some professional IOUs, obtaining permission to take a
few days off after business to visit Gordon and his family.

As I returned home to pack, I began to wonder how I
would be able to have a constructive time with him. I knew
that if I insulted him, all would be lost. Suddenly an awful
feeling came down on me from nowhere. I began to feel
trapped, smothered, hemmed-in, as if I were in a hot, black
pit with infinitely high walls. Yet I had the feeling that I was
not in the pit, but Gordon was.

Mother had told of having such sympathetic sensations

during the Vietnam War. On more than one occasion, she had been driven by awful feelings to pray for Gordon's safety. As she and Gordon had compared notes after his return from war, they saw that her prayer time had matched moments of extreme danger for him. We believed in our family that God ultimately had charge of such things. We didn't understand them, but we didn't reject them just because we couldn't wrap our minds around them, either.

Unlike Mom's Vietnam dread, the thing I felt for Gordon now seemed to threaten more than his life. It carried with it a sense of infinite separation. I sensed my brother's soul as if floating weightlessly, cut loose in a trackless void. Ultimate silence surrounded him as well as a pernicious sense of evil. The strength of the sensation carried with it, oddly, a smell: a dead sulfurous odor. In its presence, I felt like I might throw up.

"God," I prayed, kneeling at the bedside, "I feel like Gordon is going to hell. What is going on?"

As I waited for some kind of answer, I searched my thoughts. By this time in my life, especially following my studious years at Bible college, I knew my position on this subject well. I did not believe my brother was going to hell. Like me, as a child he had prayed the sinner's prayer, which had made us more than sons of Griz—we were sons of God. This belief was based on John 1, verse 12: "As many as received Him, to them He gave the right to become children of God, to those who believe in His name." If Gordon was a child of God, then no matter how he lived, he might receive punishment but he would never lose his place in the family of God. The Bible expressed this idea for me in Psalm 89, verses 30 through 33:

> If his sons forsake My law and do not walk in My judgments, if they break My statutes and do not keep My commandments, then I will punish their transgressions with the rod, and their iniquity with stripes. Nevertheless My lovingkindness I will not utterly take from him, nor allow My faithfulness to fail.

In spite of my belief that Gordon was a spiritual son of God whose soul was secure, the feeling of damnation had overwhelmed me anyway. "How can this be?" I asked.

As if in reply, the words of Griz on the telephone flashed back to me, "He's not living for God." In our family, that phrase had always amounted to a judgment of damnation. Dad may not have exactly meant it that way, but that is how the statement had come to us through childhood. Griz had always preached that a person could be saved by grace and then lose his salvation by neglecting it. That is why for so many years I had lived feeling saved when I acted good and damned for the slightest wrong. Griz could quote his share of Scriptures to back up the way he believed. Verses like Luke 12:45-46:

> But if that servant says in his heart, "My master is delaying his coming," and begins to beat the male and female servants, and to eat and drink and be drunk, the master of that servant will come on a day when he is not looking for him, and at an hour when he is not aware, and will cut him in two and appoint him his portion with the unbelievers.

The awful thing I felt about Gordon fit the words "appoint him his portion with the unbelievers." In my private experience, I wondered if perhaps the ultimate fear driving both of us all these years had been this unbearable fear of damnation. What could be worse?

Since I firmly disagreed with Griz and believed Gordon's soul was secure, I wondered why I now felt otherwise? I quickly came to grips with the fact that no matter how I believed in my head, my emotions still belonged to my childhood years. That parental tie had not been broken, even after all this time away from home; even over the great distances that now separated our family. I had to accept the strength of our family tie, for both good and bad. It could overpower even my adult beliefs.

So how should I respond? I wondered. Finally, I reasoned this way: I could not afford to argue against something as important as the destiny of my brother's eternal soul. I dismissed my beliefs and prayed according to my feelings, asking God for Gordon's salvation.

After ten minutes of this, as suddenly as it had come, the feeling of damnation left. In the great relief that followed, I heard a quiet inner voice speak to me with piercing clarity: "*Never pray for Gordon's soul again. From now on, be his brother.*"

I got up and walked around the apartment for several minutes, shaking my head, marvelling at the intense ordeal I had just passed through. Who could solve these mysteries? Whether I had prayed rightly or wrongly for my brother's soul, I felt sure God had given me the answer to my prayer. I immediately committed to obeying the inner voice; I would be a brother to Gordon. My current plans for visiting him were perfectly in line with this instruction.

With that, I resumed packing.

Gordon seemed expectant and happy to see me, but the sight of his unkempt long hair and beard caused me to feel unsure of realizing my high hopes. He wore blue jeans and a sleeveless Army shirt, unbuttoned to the waist. His look fit the image of the Vietnam vets the TV news kept showing as they gathered in Washington, D.C., protesting their treatment.

As the evening wore on, Cheryl and his daughter and young sons went to bed, leaving us alone. We sat together for hours in a trashy tack room of their rental house near the confluence of the Umatilla and Columbia Rivers. Scattered boots and jeans-adhering-to-cow-dung had been flung typically about. The old mountain saddle we had worked for, fifty-fifty, sat in a corner, prompting a good laugh. I jokingly told him that I never recalled receiving payment for my half. We relived some old times, including our litany of marksmanship.

He rolled a marijuana cigarette and lit it, offering me a hit.

"No thanks."

He nodded, inhaled, and asked about my work.

"Oh, writing mainly, producing, directing," I answered. "The money is nothing great yet. I'm still earning my stripes, but I'll tell you something: it is great to be doing the thing I was born to do. Don't ask me to pick strawberries again."

He chuckled at the memory. "Or preach either. You didn't do too good at that, as I recall."

"Right," I said. I asked him about his work.

He discarded the first cigarette, then leaned back, tapping out a Marlboro before answering. "Oh, a little of this and a little of that. Carpentry, fence building." He lit up the smoke, inhaling deeply. "You'd be surprised, I'm getting into real estate around here."

I nodded, but my imagination would not leave the illegal possibilities alone. An awful lot could be read between the lines here.

After an awkward silence the time seemed right to talk of my turnaround years in Arizona. I announced as much, and to my surprise, Gordon sat forward, seemingly eager to hear. It is a rare and wonderful thing to pass on hard-earned lessons to someone hungry to receive them. Gordon really was. I began to explain the principles and priorities I had learned in the desert school of hard knocks.

"Willpower is good," I said, "but, you know, it can put you in the ditch pretty fast. But when you take in good information and make decisions based on principles and priorities, then willpower starts to work better for you."

After a moment I added, "Bottom line, Gordy, we're talking about growing up. Somehow in all our thrashing around these past years, we've had to go back and pick up some lessons we missed along the way."

He nodded. "I really admire what you've done, little brother," he said. "You've really made a difference in your life, and I'm proud of you for it."

This compliment seemed a bit heavy on my shoulders.

If I accepted it at face value, Gordon would no doubt require that I live up to it. In the wee hours of the morning I looked at him and unloaded my soul. "Gordon, I would be wrong to say to you that I have made all of these changes on my own. I've had help. Specifically, I've had help from above. There has been a real spiritual dimension—"

"Don't talk to me about God!" he erupted. "God is *bull!*"

His ferocity shocked me. I fell into a dumbstruck silence. My first feeling was one of revulsion that he would curse at the mere mention of God. My mind flew back to just a few days ago when the little voice had spoken with such clarity: "*Never pray for Gordon's soul again.*" At this moment I wanted to do nothing more than pray for his soul. But the voice had unmistakably said *never*. While I was still wondering about this, a scriptural memory came to mind. I visualized Peter cursing, denying Christ three times on the night of the crucifixion. Perhaps, I thought, Peter and Gordon had both been wrestling a very forgivable crisis. They didn't need a sermon, they needed a brother—and it just so happened that those words were the other half of my instructions: *Be his brother.*

"I'm sorry, Gordon," I said. "Really, you didn't need to hear any of that from me."

"Naw, it's OK," he said, lighting a fresh cigarette. "I don't know why I got so excited."

"Well, there could be a lot of reasons," I offered. "Maybe even some good ones."

I could see that he had grown distant. We needed to get close again so that I could finish what I really had to say.

As I wrestled with how to begin, thankfully he broke the silence. "Well, what was that you were telling me about willpower? That sounded good."

"Right. Willpower." My mind raced, looking for common ground here. The next subject on my mind would not be willpower, but fear.

"Remember the lesson you gave me on the cliff a few miles up river from here, when you did that swan dive? Remember how you told me you wouldn't let fear keep you from doing anything you decided to do?"

He took a long, uncomfortable drag on his cigarette and nodded.

"Look around you. Is this your swan dive? Is this what you decided to do with your life?"

His eyes narrowed at me in a way that told me I had just skated onto very thin ice. He mashed out the new cigarette on a cowboy boot.

Feeling the whole conversation teetering dangerously like a vial of TNT, I plunged ahead, hoping for the best. "Is this the place you want to raise your kids? Are you living the kind of example you want them to follow?"

At this, he seemed to freeze, inside and out. This one had cut him to the heart; he loved those kids.

"What is your dream, Gordon? What is the legacy you want to leave your children? How do you want to be remembered? This can't be it."

He cleared his throat and squirmed as if deciding whether or not to belt me out the door. Then he straightened his gaze at me. "You hit it on the head, brother. This ain't it."

I nodded, feeling a growing elation inside. My gamble seemed ready to pay off. "Remember, you told me life was not about fear but about willpower? There was a lot of truth in that, but you see, big brother, I think there is something you are still scared of. So scared, in fact, that you let it keep you here."

At this point he seemed to stop breathing.

"I believe you are scared to death of failing at the thing you love the most." I had no way of knowing if I was right about this. It was a guess based on my own experience, but in a sense, everything I had to say depended on its being true.

Gordon's eyes remained downcast. He had settled against the wall with his arms crossed, not accustomed to hearing anything so straight from his younger brother. But I could see very well that he was taking it in, not letting it pass. His jaw worked. His thoughts were in motion.

Might as well finish, I decided. "You know, it's easy enough to fail at a war you didn't start. Blame the government for screwing up Vietnam. You're out of it clean. It's easy enough to fail at a ranch job you could just as easily do without, because what is that to you? The owners and managers are just a bunch of hypocrites. They don't really care about the quality of ranching. But what about your dream? That's a different thing altogether, isn't it? If you fail at that, you've got no one to blame but yourself, and that's a whole lot to put on the line."

The silence in the room grew warm. The words had found their mark, I could feel it.

"That's not a lot to put on the line," he mused, almost speaking to himself, "that's everything."

I waited a few precious seconds before concluding. "So, what is it you would love to do more than anything else in the world? What is your dream?"

Slowly, I could feel his perception permanently shift in that squalid little anteroom. After a time, he grimaced a reluctant, appreciative smile and nodded his agreement again and again, as if the whole picture kept falling more and more together before his eyes, dawning like a red western sunrise.

"Mark this day, little brother," he said quietly. "I know my dream. Know it well. My dream is to have a hunting outfit in the Rocky Mountains, in the Bitterroot Wilderness over there in Idaho. No more working for compromised, two-bit, tax write-off ranchers. I even know an outfit that's for sale. The owner lives on the Nez Perce Reservation, a place called Kooskia. I've been thinking I'd sell everything out here and go make an offer, but I've been holding back—and you're right, I have been afraid. But I'll make you this promise—no more excuses. I'll put myself on the line for it, beginning tomorrow."

Whatever weaknesses Gordon might have had, I knew that failing to keep his word was not among them. Our regard for each other grew to a whole new level that night. We were not acting like two opposite brothers anymore, but like men.

Within months of our meeting he had sold everything he owned in eastern Oregon, and had borrowed the rest, to buy that hunting outfit in Idaho. In midsummer he telephoned me in North Carolina—a call that began regular telephone contact between us—to share the new enthusiasm this challenge had brought into his life.

And so, the picture I had snapped of Gordon on that rocky Idaho ridge in 1980 had validated that late night discussion in Oregon, three years before. The photograph had captured my brother Gordon, outfitter and cowboy, living his dream with no excuses.

THE HUNT

Two days of hunting had passed in the Idaho wilderness. The usual evening campfire blazed in a rock-lined pit. Four-wall tents glimmered ghostly white in the outer ring of firelight. Griz and Uncle Bob emerged from the cook tent, having finished washing the dishes. We had all enjoyed a pot of venison chili with pan-baked cornbread. The wranglers walked in from the spring, after their nightly routines with livestock, and Gordon settled beside Cheryl. I had shot several rolls of film that day and, after reloading, now cleaned my zoom lens by lantern light. Each of us nursed weary leg muscles as we sat on stools and stumps, trading stories.

"I came on a bull in the willows," Jerry said, "only one problem . . ."

He waited until someone asked, "What's that?"—ac-

cording to the ancient and accepted rules of campfire storytelling etiquette.

"He was a bull *moose*!"

"Wrong kind of bull for sure," Griz chuckled.

"Yeah," Gordon warned, "you shoot one of my moose
and I'll send you home early."

"Moose, let's see now," Jerry ventured, "they're the
ones with the saddles and bridles, right?"

"Very funny."

"Hey," Tim jumped in, scratching his head before replacing his Mongolian hat, "I came down the hill up there
about dark and here were these two little bear cubs clinging
to a tree right in front of me. Cutest critters I've ever seen,
and so I start a little diplomacy, talking to 'em and carrying
on, you know, and pretty soon I get to thinking, 'Hey, what
am I doing here?' These little fur balls have charmed the
socks off me, but they've got a momma around here somewhere and she's bound to be a tyrant. I vamoosed myself
on out of there."

"Lots of bear up here," Gordon commented.

More vocalized reactions around the fire. Grunts and
uh-huhs mostly.

Grunts, snorts, crude-sounding words like skeedaddled,
vamoosed, scrammed, spoofed, critters, buggers, gutted,
boggled, bungled, rigged, cinched, screeched, howled, and
the like are considered valuable contributions in the rules
of campfire storytelling etiquette. Perhaps the mixed aroma
of coffee and wood smoke does it. Or the snapping and
popping of embers, with coyotes howling in the distance.
Whatever it is, it tends to transform the tenderfoot into a

timberbeast. This primitive vocabulary is known to have escaped the mouths of even the most refined of the species around a campsite blaze.

"I tell you what boggles me," Uncle Dick said. "These woods are bone dry. The elk are getting out way ahead of us. Might as well stay in camp."

This comment left an uneasy tension in the air. Especially for Gordon, who felt pressured to lead us to a kill, though Dick told the pure truth.

"Feel free to stay in camp," Gordon said. Then, after an awkward silence, he added, "I'll tell you what, though, if we don't have meat hangin' by Thursday I'll take any of you with the legs for it down to a spike camp in the hidey-hole. That's where we got that six-by-nine bull. You saw that trophy at Indian Hill on the way in, didn't you?"

We had all been excited by the sight of this trophy bull in base camp. The antlers, scored by a Ft. Worth hunter just prior to our hunt, had measured ten and one-half inches around the base and stood more than four feet tall. The stuff of dreams.

I sensed that Gordon had brought up the trophy only to remind us that big bulls did inhabit his Bitterroot forests, even though we were having trouble finding them. He had been hurt by Dick's mention of the scarcity of game. Dick, Dad's middle brother who lived in Albuquerque, hunted elk normally in the San Juan Range of Colorado. He seemed eager to compare Idaho unfavorably with his Colorado haunts. Gordon felt pride in his selected hunting territory. Most of all, he had hoped his family would have the most successful hunt of the season. Unfortunately, such things cannot be guaranteed.

Griz piped up to change the subject, "Say boys . . ."

Most anyone who knew him could tell by the tone of his voice that we were about to be spoofed.

"How'd you like those sourdough flapjacks this mornin'?"

We chimed in with hearty approval, still wondering how we were being set up. Some said they thought that they had been the best yet.

Griz and Bob looked at one another and chuckled mysteriously.

"Should I tell 'em, Bob?"

"Naw, it's too early." Bob shook his head, pretending that we would have no interest in hearing it—a storytelling ploy designed to pique our desire to hear more.

"Say Dick," Gordon said casually, "do you still know how to rig a hangin' noose?"

"Darn right. You got a handy tree?"

"Not far from here."

"Oh well," Bob jumped back in, "why don't you go on ahead and tell 'em, Griz. Rather than hang us, maybe they'll only banish us."

Looking around the fire circle I could see glances of suspicion flying this way and that as each hunter's imagination tried to anticipate the coming ruse. We knew that Dad and Bob had arisen hours before daylight to separate a new starter from the batch of sourdough and to prepare the pancake batter from the remainder. Starter amounted to a container of fermented dough that would, in turn, be used to start, or ferment, a flour and water mixture, turning the whole batch into sourdough in about eight hours. Each time the dough was used to make bread, biscuits, or, in this case, pancakes, a portion would be returned to a small crock to be used as a future starter. Dad's starter had reputedly been initiated by real sourdough gold miners during Alaska's Klondike gold rush almost one hundred years ago. Its forebears, and Sourdough Griz, had kept it alive by maintaining a continuous crock. This history, if it could be trusted, added to the romance of the food experience.

"Well, boys—and Cheryl—here's the way it is," Griz began, using a dramatic style that he normally reserved for the pulpit. "It appears that today we add another chapter to the colorful history of this sourdough starter. One of the delights of fermentation, as you know, is the sweet smell that fills the room, or in this case the tent, where the batch is in process. At one time or another in your lives, each of you has, no doubt, taken a turn at removing the towel covering the crock and dipping a finger into that sweet smelling batter."

"Uh-huh."

Indeed, we recalled the experience. The results to the tongue were the opposite of the sweet expectations raised by the aroma. This was so, because the batter progressively developed a liqueur on top as it fermented. Unless mixed and cooked properly in a recipe, the raw sourdough gruel had the taste and roughly the same potency as jet fuel.

"Last night, as near as we can tell," Dad went on, fighting to contain his mirth, "a family of mice became irresistibly drawn to our sweet-smelling mixture."

"No."

Several around the fire erupted with various forms of retching, suddenly imagining the pancakes they had eaten that morning in a new light.

"Don't tell us they left their calling cards?"

"As a matter of fact," Griz roared, "they did." Then, gaining his composure, he added, "Bob figured that if we just fished those little nuggets out of there, who would know, you know?"

"Blame it on me," Bob protested.

"You didn't throw the whole batch out?" Cheryl asked.

"Would you have waited another twenty-four hours for your sourdoughs?" Dad asked.

"Well, I might have," Cheryl replied, adding, "I suppose it would depend on how cleanly the 'calling cards' had been removed."

"We're not just talking calling cards, here," Bob tattled. "We're talking the whole salesman."

We protested loudly, imagining a mouse in our pancake dough. "Yes," Bob continued. "After fishing out the little chocolate chips, I look over and Griz holds up a little piker by the tail, all covered with batter. 'Here's Mickey,' he says, 'drunk his-self to death on sourdough booze.'"

"Went to heaven happy," Gordon laughed.

Bob continued to play out the predawn scene. "Next thing I know, Griz pulls Minnie and her kids from the batter. Now, put yourselves in our shoes; what would you do?"

"Throw it out," several yelled.

"Not Sourdough Griz," Bob replied. "He figured a one-hundred-year-old tradition was at stake. So he extracts another starter from that tub, and so, well, then he sorta figured what was good for the starter was good for the pancakes. And in that case, we decided, what was the point in sayin' anything?"

About that time Dick slipped away without explanation to the cook tent.

"Yeah," Dad defended, "I think I got everything relevant out of that batter. Besides, what was it you were all saying about those pancakes a minute ago? Huh? The best yet?"

We had been duly spoofed, tricked into complimenting Dad's mouse-fouled sourdoughs. In camping situations, we had all compromised our kitchen standards on more than one occasion, but this incident topped them all.

Dick returned to the fire circle with the starter crock. He carefully opened it, examining it by firelight, sniffing beneath the lid.

"What are you hunting for, Dick? Fresh meat?" Tim taunted.

"Might be the only thing we kill up here," he returned cynically. Then he looked up, poker-faced. "I take an occasional drink now and again, as you all know. To a drinking man the question that looms large here is, how long did it take those little critters to die?"

"Oh," Cheryl said in mock sympathy, "do you think they suffered?"

"What he's gettin' at," Gordon interjected, "is, he knows that a man can't drink for too long before making a trip to the woods, see? How long did these critters drink before they drowned? That's the question."

"Right," Dick returned. "You've got to ask yourself

what fraction of what percent of Sourdough Griz's one-hundred-year-old starter here is now mouse tinkle?"

More laughs, retches, and moans shot upward around the fire, mingled with the popping of embers and the smell of coffee. Somewhere in the night a coyote answered.

(May it here be noted that the sourdough starter story—true in each and every detail—though perhaps offensive to some, lies perfectly within the ancient and accepted rules of campfire storytelling etiquette . . . and Griz's one-hundred-year-old starter is still earning rave reviews wherever he travels.)

The allotted ten days of our hunting trip counted down without mercy. The weather remained glorious, but as Dick had stated at the campfire, good weather means poor elk hunting. Gordon had warned us in advance that we would be risking fair weather at the end of the bugle season. But he figured he knew his country well enough to beat the odds and get us close to some trophies in the deep timber pockets. In fact, late in the week he had taken a few of us into the hidey-hole, as he had promised, where Sourdough Griz missed a shot at a magnificent six-by-six bull.

After the botched shot, Gordon and I had stood rooted to the ground in disbelief. We stared at one another trying to put it into perspective. The great outdoorsman Griz, who had taught us everything we knew about hunting, had shown himself to be quite fallible. What had happened? Where were the family bragging rights? The "head-shot, neck-shot, running shot at two hundred yards" boasts? In our youth we had regarded Dad as our benchmark in the woods, and though we knew better now, for our own reasons we wanted it to always stay that way.

"Aw, it can happen to anybody," Gordon said suddenly, the first to contact reality. "Believe me, unless you are at the top of your shooting form, these animals will get the drop on you." He had already shaken off his visible disappointment and now busied himself making new hunting plans.

But it seemed the elk enjoyed the advantage over us no matter what strategy we tried. The weather had stopped the bugling cold, so we could no longer locate bulls by their mating calls. The ground remained tinder dry. Even in thick timber we snapped twigs and spooked our quarry out of reach of our guns. Every night the campfire heard more tales of frustration.

Yet I remained busy with my secret mission; loading roll after roll of Kodachrome, shooting several hundred pictures of Indian summer's riot of color in Nez Perce country. I shot camp activity, riding, hunting, flora, and those miraculously speckled eastern brook trout we pulled from the high lakes for supper—and for breakfast, and occasionally for lunch.

Toward the end of the week as we sat around the fire one night, Gordon popped out his whiskey flask and "spiced" his coffee. Most of the others had gone to their sleeping tents. The fire burned low. He held out the flask to me. "Have some?"

"Yeah, sure." It seemed part of the wilderness experience to me. The night was cold; the coffee and whiskey would warm the innards. Perhaps it was another way to celebrate my brother's life, a way to affirm him, a way to be close to him.

But something else hit me as I held out my cup for the additive. Sourdough Griz had not yet retired to his sleeping bag. He watched from across the glowing embers in the fire pit. I knew that any compromise with "drink" offended him. He had embraced teetotalism and had expected his boys to do the same. I had found the Bible to speak clearly against drunkenness, but a drink or two of whiskeyed coffee at the campfire, at least in my estimation, remained a far cry from scriptural drunkenness. I sipped.

"Time for me to hit the hay," Griz said. "See you boys in the morning." Off he went toward his tent.

Had I offended Dad? I wondered. It felt like it. Perhaps I should have been more careful. I resolved inwardly to be more respectful of him next time around. Who could blame Griz for living up to his own standards? His beliefs defined him.

The smoking embers that had once been a roaring fire glowed nearly out now. Gordon, Cheryl, and I remained alone, sipping our fortified coffee. In the distance another coyote howled. Looking up, I could see a blanket of stars shedding down more icy white light than a tenderfoot can imagine. With the pollution of artificial light in the city sky, I pondered, we can't see stars this way in the civilized world.

Gordon interrupted my thoughts, clearing his throat as if he were about to speak. I looked at him and saw that he stared into the hot coals. "If anything ever kills me up here," he said, "it'll be a mule." He took another sip and continued to stare.

I felt irritated that he would spoil the moment with such a dark thought. But I remembered the inner voice that had told me to keep quiet. Something beyond the obvious seemed to be at work here. I probed with caution. "What do you mean?"

"Mules are cantankerous, unpredictable animals, and for some reason they've got it in for me. Can't figure 'em. I mean, it's really weird. If I die up here it will be by a mule."

"Well, get rid of 'em," I blurted. It seemed the only right thing to say.

"Can't," he replied. "A mule's worth three horses in these mountains."

"You mean, this is a bottom line business decision?"

"Yep."

I fished around for my true feelings and finally spoke them. "Bottom line can take a flyin' leap. A hundred mules ain't worth you, brother."

He smiled an appreciative smile, took a final sip of coffee, tossed the dregs hissing into the coals, and announced his bedtime.

Our final morning in the mountains saw a diffused dawn cross a canopy of deep clouds above us. A misty rain had been falling for hours, quieting the forests. Gordon stowed gear and loaded packs with a bitter expression on his face, wondering aloud if "God had it in for him" to send the good hunting weather just as we were leaving. I watched in silent sympathy, feeling helpless. Not one of us had bagged one of those Bitterroot trophy bulls.

For me, the process of breaking camp carried a mood of melancholy anyway. As I watched, I reflected about the reasons for it: As flatlanders, we had entered an unfamiliar wilderness and had carved out a comfort zone of tents among the evergreens. Routines had been established. We had memorized the path to the spring so that we could walk to it in the black of night. We had learned to brush our teeth out there with water cold enough to crack enamel. We had learned to find the outdoor toilet in the dark, defrost the seat, and use it without bolting every time a coyote howled. For ten days we had eaten our predawn pancakes accompanied by numberless mugs of coffee and hot chocolate, returning each evening to chili, spaghetti, stew, steaks, and storytelling. We had learned to go naked into an Indian sweat lodge and use a fir branch to sprinkle moisture on glowing, white-hot stones until we were steaming enough to douse ourselves with springwater for a squeaky clean rinse. We had claimed individual stumps and logs in that primitive fire circle. They would remain now, the only sign of our having been there. We had learned to crawl into impossibly cold sleeping bags hoping, praying, believing, and finally knowing, that the synthetic fibers would live up to their temperature ratings. The straw beneath us had conformed exactly to the curl of our sleeping bodies. Too soon, it seemed to me—much too soon—all of this familiarity was being dismantled.

Watching Gordon bend over a pack, I reflected on the fact that this hunt had taken on a life of its own. A hunt like no other. It had been a combination of all the experiences we had shared, the personalities of Griz, Dick, Tim, Bob,

Jerry, Gordon, and Cheryl. In subtle ways it included the members of our families waiting back at home, our personal histories—"backstories," as the screenwriter calls them. It had been the trails we walked alone and together, the maps we searched, thickets we entered, the sourdough pancakes eaten and the stories told. It had been the time, the place, and all of the circumstances beyond our control, including the weather. All of it had been fine.

I believed that Gordon's mission had been accomplished. He should know it, and nothing should take it from him. His success had never been measured by the weather, the killing of an elk, or the mounting of a trophy head. It had been in the art of the journey, the strong work of his expert fingers on the pack, in the months of preparation, of thinking about us, of dreaming and planning. It had been in the intentions of his heart, well-masked beneath that desperado beard. It had been in the whiskey and the coffee, and in a tin dipper of clean spring water, offered without the asking.

Smiling to myself now, I felt warmed among the clicking of tent stakes, the zip of pack rope, the grunts of wranglers and the stirring of impatient horses around us. In the gentle rain itself, my melancholy melted away into gratitude.

Remembering the instructions of a professional photographer back in North Carolina, "Don't hesitate to shoot 200 Ektachrome in bad weather," I hurried to load my camera with the stuff he had prescribed for these conditions. I started shooting again.

We rode out of the great Rocky Mountains in silence. I continued to work for as many photographs of our group in the moody rain as my mind could conceive. No one commented about my photographic antics anymore—galloping ahead, dismounting at times, lagging behind, removing my gloves again and again to shoot this angle, then that. I had let it out that I planned a Christmas album from the hunt. They all liked that idea just fine.

At one point on the seven-hour ride, I noticed that the rain dripping from our hat brims had turned to snow at tree top level. The effect enchanted me. Autumn earth tones, appearing at horseback level, gradually transformed into a ghostly white above. Like an expensively printed Christmas card, a distant line of frosted tree tops seemed embossed against the whitened sky.

An open hillside loomed ahead where the entire effect could be captured, I thought. Our horseback trail climbed through that hillside in a series of switchbacks. This configuration would lead the eye to examine the spectrum of changing colors from bottom to top. Of course, the picture would not work without horses and riders in the switchbacks. I dismounted and waited for them to reach the place.

They rode past my position, and I raised the camera in cold-numbed hands. Everything I hoped for appeared beautifully in the viewfinder as the group paused to rest on the hillside. *Click, click, click, click,* I worked the shutter over and over again, knowing that I had captured something special. Perhaps the most evocative moment of our ride. Whooping it up, I remounted and galloped ahead of the group again.

A short time later, we entered a long, tunnel-like forest trail where the same weather effect appeared even more pronounced. A few falling snowflakes showed up in stark relief against the dark tree trunks below. Again I dismounted as the others passed on my left.

Then I noticed that my film winder would not respond to the pressure of my fingers. To my preoccupied mind, that meant that I had wound off the Ektachrome but had forgotten to change to a fresh roll. I opened the back of the camera—and snapped it immediately shut. The film had not been rewound. Perhaps all of the precious pictures I had just taken had been destroyed, exposed to the light. A four-letter word burst from my mouth with great force.

Just then I looked up directly into the face of The Reverend Sourdough Griz, riding past me at that very moment. *Why does my guardian angel arrange these things?* I wondered. How could I explain my use of foul language to a man who used it before I was born but never since? He certainly had never heard this word from me before—not that I hadn't said it.

As I grimly reloaded, the horses and riders continued on their weary way through the tunnel of trees before me. Raising the camera, I focused on Dad's retreating back. "Hey, Griz!" I hollered.

He turned in the saddle. *Click.*

I lowered the camera. "Sorry, Dad. I forgot myself. It's just that I am really into these pictures, you know? I got a little frustrated because I ruined some film, and . . ."

Knowing Dad, my apology had washed just fine. Straight-up apologies always did with him. To say, "I'm sorry," meant that the guilty party had repented, period. However, to go on to explain that frustration had driven me to cursing did not amount to any kind of excuse in his mind. I could tell that by the way he turned forward again, riding away without so much as a nod of absolution.

At base camp we dined together one last time before returning to our automobiles and driving away to our various places in the civilized world. Everyone repeated their condolences to Gordon for the weather and the lack of elk on the hunt. He seemed gracious but grim.

No such grimness dampened my spirits. Inwardly, I warmed with renewed excitement. I had done the impossible; I had obeyed the inner voice. For ten days I had said nothing—absolutely nothing about myself, my career, or accomplishments. Instead, I had celebrated the hunt and my brother's life in photographs. I could hardly wait to get my negatives developed back home and view the results. All of the good-bye gloom I would normally feel at such a time had been replaced with anticipation for the task ahead: assembling those Christmas photo albums over the next two months.

Suddenly, as we ate, Gordon began asking me questions. Any new screenplays? How's the novel project going?

This is how it is supposed to be, I thought. Ignore myself, and Gordon will ask about my accomplishments when the time is right. Sure beats bragging. But I had enjoyed not talking about myself so much, I felt reluctant to start. I answered more hesitantly than ever in my life, playing down the potentials of my new projects, quickly changing the subject.

About then, a new idea struck me. I excused myself and

went to my pack, returning with the book *Writing for the Outdoor Market*. I had packed it in Carolina and had not thought of it since. I handed it to Gordon.

"What's this?"

"It's for you. Keep it. There's a story behind it, Gordy. Remember old Mr. Smith from English Comp? Bulldog High?"

"You don't forget a guy like him."

"He said you were the most talented writer in the family. Said you wrote like Hemingway. Now, I say it's time you dusted off that talent and put it to some good use."

"You do?"

"I do. Not only that, you could give your business some free national exposure in a hunting magazine. Heck, they'd pay you for the story of that six-by-nine bull you brought in before our hunt."

He looked the book over and nodded. "You know? That's the truth. Maybe I should write it up this winter in Kooskia when we're all snowed in."

"Absolutely. That book will tell you what the magazines are looking for, how much they pay, how long to make the article and stuff like that. The main thing is, you could tell one fine story and you know it."

"Thank you, brother. I'll do it." He put the book on the table beside his plate and patted it.

As sure as the smell of frying bacon I knew that he would write that story. And I figured something else, too; he would prove to be the most talented writer in the family. The nice part about it was, for the first time in our competitive lives it would be perfectly all right with me.

Following the meal, we posed for final pictures before saying our good-byes.

"Well, big brother," I said, "all good things must end."

"Yep." He stuck out his hand and shook mine firmly.

"I got some great pictures. I'll be sendin' them to you."

"Thanks."

"And one thing more," I said, looking him in the eye, "I want you to know the truth, here. I have enjoyed every minute of this hunt. Couldn't ask for more. I want to thank you, really, for giving me the greatest outdoor adventure of my life."

Tears sprang up in his eyes. What's more, one squeezed out and ran down his dusty beard. He didn't even try to hide it from me, the crybaby he had been embarrassed to take anywhere as a kid. He stood there, as if momentarily uncertain, then suddenly rasped, "I love you, brother." And he lunged forward, grabbing me in a bearlike embrace.

Moments like these cannot be purchased. Cannot be predicted or arranged. Perhaps they are only possible when the still small voice speaks. Gordon had never said "I love you" to me in all our lives. Nor had he brought himself to hug me before now. I hugged him back as best I could, seeing how his strong arms had nearly already deflated my lungs. We pulled back from our embrace, holding each other by the shoulders, smiling through blurred vision and feeling things brothers are created to feel but rarely do.

He slapped my shoulder hard. "Get on out of here," he laughed.

I did. I vamoosed.

THE CHRISTMAS ALBUM

I think you have a lot to be pleased with."

The voice of the photo lab rep sounded encouraging on the phone. Coming from this normally reticent professional, I knew at least some of my pictures had achieved professional standards.

"I'll be right there," I said, dropping everything in my eagerness to see them. I hurried across Charlotte to the lab.

"I've got your slides in the back room," he said, "but who's this?" He had laid the black-and-white print of Gordon on the counter top.

"That's my brother. Isn't he something?" The camera had captured the moment he and the horse had filled the viewfinder on that long Idaho ridge: a unique blend of Vietnam vet, outfitter, and poet-cowboy in his wild element—everything I had hoped to capture.

"What a character," the lab rep said. "I thought he was an actor on a movie set or something. You mean he really looks that way in real life?"

"He does. He's a hunting outfitter in the Selway-Bitterroots of northern Idaho," I said with pride.

"Well, pictures do tell a story, don't they?"

"They do."

We went to the back room to use the light table—at which time I learned what a light table was: a translucent table top with a light source behind it to illuminate photographic transparencies. Professionals use them every day. The proper viewing technique, the technician showed me, involved using a magnifying lens to inspect the details of each slide at close range.

I took the lens and bent over the series of shots he had laid out for comparison. Sure enough, Kodachrome had captured the sunlight colors, and Ektachrome, the colors seen on the rainy trip out of the mountains.

Most remarkably, one of the pictures in the series I had ruined by opening the back of the camera survived. Along its right border the film had been burned, but on the left of the frame, in a perfectly square format, the horses and riders of our pack train waited quietly in the moody rain and snow.

"This is your best shot," the lab rep said. "If I were you I would enlarge it and enter it in a contest."

When I knew for sure that he was serious, I looked more closely at the picture and grew thoughtful. It seemed incredible that after all my photographic effort on the hunt, my prizewinning shot turned out to be an accident. This, I thought, would be a good reason never to curse again. If an accident could produce my best work, then maybe it hadn't quite been an accident after all. Maybe my guardian angel had seen to it that I learned not to take myself so seriously. Getting angry and frustrated enough to utter profanity was just another way to charge through life without opening my eyes and ears to the greater realities around me.

In the coming weeks I selected and assembled the photo albums. It only seemed fitting to make the opening page from the enlargement of the black-and-white portrait of Gordon. The other enlarged showpiece, of course, was made from my accidental prizewinner.

The albums were ready well before Christmas, and I packaged and sent each one with instructions to open immediately. All the families called during the holidays to express their appreciation. Finally, Gordon called.

"You were right about that picture on the ridge out by Otter Butte, Steve. I have to say it's my favorite all-time shot. We plan to use the whole album in our booth at hunting shows next year. And by the way," he added, "I'm at work on a magazine story about that six-by-nine bull. I'll let you know how it turns out."

"Great," I said.

■

1981 became a very busy year for me as I launched my own small television production business. Late in August, I received a call from Gordon, very excited. The September issue of *Sports Afield* magazine featured his article about the six-by-nine bull!

"They put a picture of you and me on the opening page of the article," Gordon said. "It's only fitting, brother. You gave me that outdoor writing book."

"Yeah, but you dusted off that talent of yours and made something out of it. Congratulations. When a national magazine publishes your very first attempt at writing, it proves you've got what it takes. Most writers go through a lot of rejection before they do what you've done."

I hurried to the nearest grocery chain and bought out their stock of the September issue of *Sports Afield*. Several copies would be squirreled away in my files and others would be handed out for bragging about my talented brother.

I opened one and found the article. On the title page, a picture Cheryl had snapped of Gordon and me preparing to enter the deep hidey-hole in search of elk appeared just beside the title, "Elk Chronicle: Family tradition helps an Idaho guide lead his client on a successful hunt for a trophy."

At home, I called him again, with the article in front of me.

"We submitted a group of pictures," he explained. "I hoped they would pick this one of you and me, and it turns out, that's the one they chose. I guess it's the good Lord's way of thanking you for getting me into this, brother."

Cheryl spoke up from the phone extension, telling me proudly what her husband would not say: "The editors didn't just accept this article, they said that it was the truest and most gripping description of an elk hunt they had ever read."

"I'm not surprised," I replied. "Old 'Cue Ball' Smith spotted Gordon's talent back in high school, and he obviously knew what he was talking about. I can't wait to read it myself."

After hanging up the phone, I sat down and read "Elk Chronicle," marveling at Gordon's pungent descriptions and realistic dialogue. The writing seemed far above standard for a hunting magazine. It was literature, with universal human themes deftly woven throughout a story of hunting. No doubt it would have earned another A+ on Smith's scale of excellence. On mine, too.

Just before calling him again, I set the magazine down and grinned to myself, seeing a strawberry field in my memory and Gordon's impossibly bent back disappearing into the mists of glory ahead of me. He won, and it *was* all right with me. I smiled again, realizing that the impossible mission whispered to me by the still small voice had changed my life.

UNFINISHED BUSINESS

L ess than thirty days later, fall hunting season commenced without me. Too busy to take time off for deer or elk, I worked late in my office over a TV commercial budget.

The phone rang. To my surprise, it was Cheryl. She said that Gordon had suffered a hunting accident. Deep in the Bitterroots after setting camps, his hand had become trapped in the loose coils of a pack rope, and he had been dragged in the dark of night. To me, this seemed impossible because I had watched him enough to know that he always took great care with pack rope. He knew it was a hazard, especially when attached to an animal. She went on to say that the offending animal had been his least favorite mule.

A mule! I remembered his words by the campfire: "*If anything kills me up here it'll be a mule.*" I wanted to reject the thought now, as I had then. It's not a serious a accident, I told myself, don't be superstitious.

Cheryl went on to explain that the mule had bolted downhill, dragging Gordon into a tree with enough force to upend the animal. "Gordon wasn't even knocked out," she said. "He didn't break the arm either, just traumatized it up to the shoulder pretty good. The worst part is, the rope coils crushed his hand and jerked a finger off."

"Ow," I yelled over the phone.

"Well, you know how that lariat rope is," she said. "It cuts like a saw blade. Anyway, he rounds up the mule and rides out of the mountains with his string, just like that."

"I sure can't imagine Gordon calling for a care flight chopper to get him out," I added dryly.

"Not him. He got himself to a Clearwater doctor about six in the morning. He's strong. Then he drove on home. We think he should be back on his feet before season's end."

"I sure hope so." I turned to examine the enlarged photo of him, now sitting proudly on my credenza. I had removed it from the photo album, framing it for permanent display. The picture revealed a detail I remembered well: Gordon's right hand remained open in the loop of the lead line, while the other held the reins. I had asked him about the exact nature of that loop, and he had explained it: "I keep it tied off so the rope won't grab my hand if some crazy mule goes nuts on the trail." Given his natural distrust for mules, I wondered how he had failed to be careful with those loose coils of rope? Maybe it had been a starless night, and he had been confused in the dark.

"What was he doing on the trail at night?" I asked.

"You know Gordon. Thinks he's superman. He had set three camps that day."

"Superman" was the nickname other Idaho wranglers had given him. During our hunt, they had told of Gordon setting an impossible working pace. He had logged more hours on the trail, they said, chopped more wood in a day, run steeper hills up and down, and held the record for the most camps set.

Forty carriers a day, I reminded myself, recalling his obsessive work ethic. He had driven himself like that all of his life, but it had caught up with him. Pushing himself along that trail at night, past the point of fatigue, he had lost his alertness and it had cost him a finger.

"Tell Gordon it's time to stop being superman," I said. "He needs to give himself, and everyone else, a break."

"He's already been told," Cheryl said. "I hope that's the main lesson to come out of this." After an uncertain pause, she added, "There is one other problem; we don't know how serious it is, but some kind of infection is bothering the wound and we're sending him up to Spokane so some specialists can look at it. We'll keep in touch."

"All right, do that," I said. "Give him my very best wishes for a speedy recovery."

"I will."

I returned to work feeling that an imaginary alarm was ringing in a distant room. It demanded that I should pay attention to it, but instead, I shrugged it off. I told myself to be thankful that this accident had taught Gordon to stop punishing himself. It would be a *good* accident in the long run, I thought, like my accidental photo taken in the snow. It would reveal an unexpected surprise someday.

In the meantime, my desk held piles of work that shouted for undivided attention. I plowed into it.

Three days later, another phone call disturbed my concentration. "You'd better get out here," Griz said.

Somehow I knew immediately that he wasn't talking about Alaska. "Where are you, Dad?"

"At the hospital in Spokane," he said. His tone of voice stunned me. It seemed far too serious. "I warn you, son, you are probably not going to get here in time."

For a moment I couldn't feel anything. Not one thing. "That's impossible," I stated. "He's not that sick."

"Son, he's more than sick. He's dying. That poison has baffled every specialist in the state of Washington. It's into his vital organs now."

I sat too stunned to speak. How could the inner voice fail to warn me? How could I have missed the seriousness of Gordon's condition? Worse yet, how could I be too late to ever see him again? "This can't be, Dad. How—how can he be dying over a simple accident like this?"

"That's the question everybody's asking, but you don't have time to think about it just now. Better do your thinking on the plane. But, prepare yourself, son. I don't think you will see your brother alive."

Dad's pronouncement was unthinkable. I flat rejected it. I would get there in time, even though I lived a continent away. That was all there was to it.

On the next Delta L1011 out of Charlotte, my stomach churned. Around me, passengers roared with laughter at

Dudley Moore and Liza Minelli frolicking through the plot of *Arthur* on the forward screen. I could not bring myself to even try to comprehend the movie. I gazed through the darkened window, praying with every ounce of my being, but the still small voice had become silent within me. A constant dread in the center of my thoughts seemed to relentlessly promise that Gordon's time had come. It remained for me to accept the inevitable, as Griz had warned.

Wrestling with that possibility, I began to bargain. I prayed that if his time had come, God would at least grant me time enough to see him one more time. "I'm telling you, God, this is *very* important," I whispered fiercely, my eyes stinging. *If God let me down in this*, I thought, *well, He just might lose a pretty darn good friend.*

These faithless thoughts opened my soul to its darker recesses. I could look inside to a rebellious place where selfishness ruled like a child-king. That seething child was so proud as to choose to live in hell rather than submit to a God who might allow my brother to die before I arrived. From this part of me, I sensed, the bitterness that destroyed like a red-eyed rage would arise to turn one tragedy into two, or more.

I reached into my Bible memory, sorting lessons Griz had taught from the pulpit, recalling Christ's words when he had prayed to be spared the crucifixion; "Nevertheless, not my will, but Yours be done." When I repeated His words, I could feel things grow right inside of me again. I also secretly hoped that my obedient praying might in some way obligate God to answer my prayer my way—by preserving my brother's life.

When the flight touched down before dawn in Seattle, I hurried to the nearest public telephone and dialed the Spokane hospital. Griz's voice choked with tears on the other end of the line. "You're too late, son."

I had been hit once with a left hook during a childhood boxing lesson. Not realizing his own strength, Griz had knocked me silly. As I had stumbled around the living room, hearing voices as if through a tunnel, his distinctive bass had cut across my consciousness: "I think that one rang your bell, son." I could hear the words again now, echoing. My skull pulsed with them like a struck tuning fork.

Reeling from the phone booth, I knew that this hard reality could not be absorbed on impact. My systems were shorting out.

"Meet the rest of the family in Idaho," I had heard Dad say before losing focus. "We'll be sending the body to Kooskia."

A gigantic choking sob rose up in my throat, but it wouldn't come out. My face burned. I returned to the booth to place the receiver on its cradle, realizing that the answer to my prayer on the plane had been a resounding *no*. I smashed the receiver a second time, as the questions—*Why didn't you tell me? Why wasn't I there?*—wrenched through my head.

As I went through the motions of booking my next flight, I began to comprehend some things. Not able to think directly about Gordon, I began to sense how death comes for every living being unexpectedly, always too soon, "like a thief in the night," as the Scripture said. Unlike the mercy and grace of living, it leaves absolutely no room for correction. Gordon is gone, I thought. What is done is done.

Over the next few hours a heavy knot formed near my solar plexus. It actually felt like a physical tumor, or a lump of phlegm. It would not go away no matter how often I swallowed, no matter how many airline coffees I drank. I coughed to dislodge it, cleared my throat, pounded a fist against it. Nothing worked. I soon realized that it was not a physical thing, but pain, the likes of which I had never known.

I could not express it. Nor deal with it. Neither could I deal with anything else happening around me. I tried to sit, but constantly fidgeted. Tried to read, could manage only a partial sentence. TV seemed a hollow joke. Could not talk to anyone in the terminal, nor on the plane to Idaho. Tried to sleep but talons of guilt clutched sharply at the ball in my chest whenever I closed my eyes for too long. I jerked awake with sudden fits and starts. Guilt? Guilt for what?

For not being there. For arriving too late.

When thoughts would focus, I wondered what I might have said at his bedside. Too late. Did he die thinking of me as the crybaby? Too late. The one who could not leap from the cliff? Too late. Afraid of the dark? Too late. Had he died trying to keep me from facing something he thought would be too tough for me to handle, like Vietnam? Anger flared in me at this possibility. "Well, then he should have known better!" I seethed under my breath.

But the word *should* no longer fit reality. Death *should* not happen, yet it does. Nothing else that touches death is quite as it *should* be ever again. Like trying to fit a jigsaw puzzle together using a stray piece from another puzzle, the word *should* would not apply where death was concerned. *Nothing can be right about death,* I thought; it is the proverbial "unrightable wrong."

Many such thoughts whirled through my mind. All of them keeping me from thinking too directly about Gordon.

I arrived in Kooskia, a collection of four dozen houses on the Nez Perce Indian Reservation near the foot of the Bitterroot Range. Snow covered the half-settled countryside along the south fork of the Selway. A small pioneer grave-yard on the edge of town had been designated as Gordon's final resting place. A funeral home several miles the other direction made preparations for his body. In the middle of town, a half block off Main Street, we gathered with Cheryl and her kids at their one-story frame house. Numbly, wearily, we attempted to sort our feelings and provide comfort if possible.

We conversed from stuffed chairs and sofas around a burlwood coffee table. While we sipped hot spiced tea and cider, we learned that my younger brother Tim, who now lived in Seattle, had been at Gordon's bedside for seven hours straight, playing guitar and singing cowboy songs. Also from Seattle, brother-in-law Jerry had come to the hospital with his wife Becky. She and Cheryl had remained with Gordon around the clock. Incredibly, Mom and Griz had arrived from Anchorage just twelve hours before the end. *They had been called at that late hour,* I thought, *why hadn't I?*

Griz shared with us how he had been drawn to Gordon's bedside in the wee hours of that final morning, as his vital signs had begun to plunge. At the same moment, I had apparently been praying to an inner silence on that jetliner. The distraught medical staff had already inserted a respirator into his mouth and were preparing a last desperate surgery when Griz walked in unexpectedly.

Gordon lay strapped to the bed, seemingly unconscious, but Dad sensed that his son was silently calling to him from across the room. His voice growing unsteady and thin in that Kooskia living room, Griz next told us that he had looked closely and could see Gordon's fingertips moving as if signaling, even though his arms were strapped down.

Griz had called out, "Son, do you want me to come over there?"

His bass voice had stopped the medical team in their tracks. As they all turned and stared, Gordon's head struggled and nodded yes.

Griz quickly crossed the room, taking his son by the hand. He had been at his share of deathbeds during more than thirty years of ministry. He had seen partings from the best to the worst: some with cursing, others crying, a few confessing. From his own collection of irrevocable moments, he knew that the final threads of life, those delicate connections that suspend someone between time and eternity, were not medical. They were heart and soul and mind and spirit. Griz knew that the sound of a familiar voice could bring one back from the brink to linger—the touch of a father's hand, a memory, a quoted Scripture, a prayer, an apology. He knew that a reconciliation at a time like this could release a dying soul to make a resolved and peaceful break with this world.

He squeezed Gordon's hand and felt a tender, warm squeeze in reply. Dad's heart leaped, wanting nothing more than a chance to talk to his son, but the time for two-way conversation had passed. The respirator had taken care of that.

Feeling a wave of regret, he recalled how that hours ago, shortly after he and Mom had arrived, Gordon had suddenly awakened, bright and full of vigor. Seeing this, Griz and the others had allowed hope for recovery to spring up inside of them. They had taken that time to talk of the position of the bed, hospital food, the hunting business, the pain, medications. Mostly small talk. At one point Griz had asked if, through his ordeal, Gordon had thought of where he would spend eternity. For the aging outdoorsman-preacher with the sad shoulders, there could be no more important question.

Gordon knew Griz well. He had answered carefully and respectfully, "I've been thinking about it for a long time, Dad. Not just here in this hospital."

Hearing Dad repeat these words to those of us gathered in Kooskia, my mind raced back four years to the last time I had mentioned God in Gordon's presence. He had exploded with rage. Apparently, the rage had covered a heart still sensitive to spiritual matters.

Griz went on. He told us that he had appreciated Gordon's reply because he knew his son would not make promises just because his life was in danger. He had lived through the carnage of Vietnam and that had not driven him to a "foxhole" conversion. Knowing that Gordon had heard the sermon about "getting right with God" a thousand times, the preacher had not pressed the matter any further at that time.

Now, everything had changed. Griz wondered if he had waited until too late. He watched his son slip in and out of consciousness. Fighting for life, then losing, fighting again, and losing. "Son, if you can hear me, will you give my hand another squeeze?"

He squeezed, and Griz thanked God that he was still there.

"I have to ask you a question, son. I know you love me, but I don't want you to answer out of love for your old dad, now. I need to know the truth. Whatever it is, I need the truth, straight up." He paused, took a breath, then asked, "If you've made your peace with God and you're really ready to meet Him, would you give my hand another squeeze right now?"

Griz felt a shock run the length of his arm. Gordon's knuckles turned white with more power than Griz thought could have remained in his decimated body. Then, as Gordon held tightly to his dad's hand, his eyes fluttered open, and he looked him in the eye, straight and clear. After several seconds, his eyes unfocused and seemed to see nothing. He relaxed and let go, lapsing again into unconsciousness.

Long after they had wheeled him away, Griz said, he had stood rooted to the spot, smiling through his tears. He kept staring at his hand bearing the imprint of that final message from Gordon.

As he finished retelling the incident in the living room in Kooskia, he held his weathered hand up again for the rest of the grieving family. The imprint was gone, but he said he could almost feel that reassuring squeeze again. His eyes grew bright with tears and spilled over. His shoulders grew taller and straighter. He smiled and choked out a whispered—"Praise God!" He knew that he would see his son again in heaven.

The rest of us didn't know quite how to respond. Dad had lived his life with a steady eye on the hereafter. We had all hoped for much more in this life. Death had cut short our planned time with Gordon, especially considering the needs of his wife and young children. It seemed impossible for us to praise God with the same depth of gratitude Griz felt.

I privately marvelled, though, realizing more deeply than ever that his beliefs had not wavered since 1949. Down to and including the moment of his firstborn son's death— even then, he had practiced what he preached. I shuddered at the enormous challenge his life presented to what could only be seen, by comparison, as my own unsteady faith.

The next morning I awakened with a real problem. A nearly red-eyed rage had taken me in the night. As with most death issues, it was probably true that my core anger was aimed at God. After all, life and death are His domain. He knows these things in advance; we don't. But instead of cursing God, I began, with less integrity, to resent those family members who had been at Gordon's bedside and had not thought of calling me sooner.

As I showered and shaved, I attempted to combat my

resentment with reason. I reminded myself that they had been cruelly tossed back and forth between doctors' opinions and their own hopes for Gordon's recovery. No one had wanted to give up hope, even at the end. My head understood all of that and accepted it, but my heart kept rising up in anger anyway.

I knew this kind of bitter emotion could spill out and infect the minds of my grieving family members. I had heard my share of funeral horror stories. God knew I didn't want to feel the anger, but I did, and it threatened the peace of my family.

Late in the day, news came that Gordon's body had arrived at the funeral home north of town. It had been prepared for a closed casket graveside service the next day. No funeral home viewing had been planned.

True to his lifestyle, we learned that he had been laid out in a rough-hewn pine coffin, nailed together at his request by Idaho wranglers. But in his final instructions he had forgotten to tell them to measure the funeral home door. The oversized box would not pass through, even after the staff had removed the hinges trying to fit it in. With repeated apologies, the funeral director telephoned to explain that he had found no other choice but to keep the body in the limousine garage.

His apologies were lost on us. Someone in the house, it might have been Uncle Dick, mentioned that "wasn't it too bad that that shiny black limousine over at the funeral home has to gather dust and bird droppings, all because Gordon's oversized coffin put it out of its shelter?" This bittersweet comment sparked a round of chuckling. Then someone else mentioned that it seemed a fitting tribute to Gordon. The free-spirited cowboy had never properly passed through the doorway of any institution in his life—"Why should he start with a funeral home?" Soon the living room was in an uproar, the children watching the adults with darkly curious eyes as if the world had suddenly gone mad; we laughed our sides sore and wiped our eyes.

That shared moment of poignancy caused something to fall into place for me. I realized that I dreaded seeing Gordon's dead body about as much as I had feared leaping from that cliff the day he had challenged me, "*Do it, you nit!*" To a degree, both challenges amounted to looking death in the face.

I knew what I had to do. Clearing my throat, I said, "I am going over to have a look at Gordon." The words fell like stones in the room.

Cheryl looked at me, surprised, then slowly her expression softened. She nodded her approval. Did she remember that we had both been with Gordon around that campfire a year ago when he had spoken of the mule? If she remembered, then perhaps she understood that, of all the family members, I should have been the one to fly to his side at the first mention of the accident. For whatever reason, I was so glad she agreed to my seeing Gordon.

"No, son," I heard Griz say. He took my arm and pulled me into an adjoining room. Lowering his voice, he said, "I don't think it's such a good idea. Your brother died real hard. The poison left him almost beyond recognition. I'm putting this nicely to say they cut him up with a lot of surgery at the end; someone else might use a different word to describe it—do you catch my drift? They didn't fix him up for viewing. That's why they nailed that lid shut. We don't want any of the family seeing him this way."

For a moment I felt like a child again, wanting to hear Griz's omniscient voice explain life and its mysteries for me. The outgrown family relationship called urgently, falsely, tempting me to simply do as I was told. But that feeling lasted only a moment.

"No, you don't understand, Dad," I said. "This is not right, the way things happened. I didn't get to say good-bye to my brother, and now I'm going to do it." Intuitively I knew this was the answer to the resentment I felt. *Stop blaming the others*, I said. *Go see your brother, no matter who objects.*

"But you have a lot of good memories, son," Griz continued. "You don't want this to spoil them."

I knew he meant well, but he had no way of knowing how this idea affected me. It also told me how much water had passed under the bridge since I had left home, more than I had time to explain. There would be time for that later. In the meantime, his words implied that my memories might be destroyed by seeing the truth. Inside, my thoughts nearly screamed, *I want the truth, I want to remember the truth, and the whole truth!* The old red-eyed rage was no threat to me now. It had found its proper place. At this moment it kept me moving steadily in the right direction, and under decent control.

I went to the living room and found Cheryl. "Would you please call the funeral home and tell them that you want them to take the lid off that pine box? I am on my way to see my brother."

As she turned toward the phone, I headed out the door.

Sourdough Griz, Tim, and Jerry grabbed their coats and hats and followed me out.

Twilight had fallen. Griz drove the icy road in silence. The fenced pastures of the Nez Perce foothills passed by like the squares of a quilted shroud, snow covered and blue cold in the dusk, stitched together with hedgerows of barren sumac and tumbleweed. Pebbles of freezing sleet rattled against the windshield as the defroster worked like a blow torch to keep our vision clear. To me it seemed another ice age had descended on Idaho; I almost wished for a year without seasons.

After a couple miles, Tim commented, "Snow came late this year."

"Yeah," Jerry agreed.

I suddenly realized that hunting season had entered its final days. "Did Gordon's hunters cancel?" I asked.

"No, son," Dad responded, "these wranglers around here all pitched in to see that his season was taken care of. Every hunter went out on schedule."

I wanted to hug those guys.

"That's nice," someone said.

"Yeah. Real nice."

The director met us at the funeral home doorway with more apologies for the location of the casket. We told him not to worry, but he couldn't seem to take our word for it. He had not known Gordon as we had.

"Just show me my brother," I told him flatly.

The man pointed to a tacky wooden stairwell in the

corner of the lobby, where all the carpeting and wallpaper ended. It led to a basement garage.

We turned and descended the stairs into a damp, cave-like room with a musty earthen floor. I could smell mildew, pinewood, and motor oil. At the bottom of the stairs, we stopped. In the middle of the room sat a huge unfinished coffin. All of rough, splintery wood. The box had heavy braces. Lariat handles. So appropriate, I thought. The lid had been removed and the freshly exposed nails caught the light from a single unfrosted bulb hanging at the end of a frayed cord above.

I stared long and hard, hearing the rush of my own blood in my ears. Not a breath of air dared stir in that place. The box remained unyieldingly silent in its naked pool of light; so silent, yet so full of my brother. Behind me, the occasional nervous clearing of throats and audible breathing told me where the others stood.

They held back as I moved forward alone. Each of them had spent time at Gordon's bedside; I had not. I began to fill with expectation as I forced my legs to move across the packed earthen floor. What did I expect? That he would rise up and greet me? No, I sensed the nearly silent voice saying to me with a chorus of angels, *"Well done. This is exactly what you are supposed to do."*

I reached the edge of the box and looked inside. The sight hit me like a blast of cold air. Immediately my eyes began pouring out hot tears. I blinked them away and they pattered across a clear plastic tarpaulin covering his naked body. Griz had told it straight: they had not prepared him for viewing.

For a moment I recognized nothing resembling my brother. But as I continued to look, I knew him. I forced myself to see the whole truth as the final tribute I owed him. My eyes took in the details of his suffering. Important details: the missing finger, the crushed hand that had been ensnared by the mule, the swollen arm seventeen inches around. The upper body discolored and bruised from the still unnamed poison. The puffy face, distorted yet recognizable, looking strangely younger shorn of its once-proud beard. The scalp, loosely sewn into place after the last futile surgery.

How could this be Gordon? How? But there was no mistake. This was my brother, thirty-four years old. Death has no respect.

As I continued to stare, the curious lump began to break up inside my chest. I knew in that moment that it had been something evil, hard, cold, puny, and cowardly. I felt all the anger and resentment toward my family leave. I knew now that those who had been by Gordon's bedside felt a more complicated pain than I felt—one they would not wish on me, nor anyone else. One that would take them many more years to properly accommodate. I could only imagine the helplessness they had felt, watching someone they loved, someone virile and vital, in his prime, as he had burned relentlessly down to the grave in a stew of virulent poison.

They tell me, in such times, that it is as if God has no voice. I can only reply that I believe in such times God has the same voice He always has. His is a quiet message—seldom shouted—and like still water, its course runs deep within. In times of suffering I believe it is often drowned beneath our howls of fear, anger, and denial—spiritual ear-stoppers I have known well enough. On our best days we seldom have ears to hear it; so many other voices amuse us. Sometimes we don't believe it when we hear it. At other times we simply don't obey the faint promptings we do hear. Then again, out of anguish, it is possible to tell God to take His voice and be gone.

Just as people have various experiences of His voice, they also find their own processes for grieving. I cannot recommend what happened next in that musty garage as I viewed my brother's corpse. But I will tell it.

Almost involuntarily, I heard my voice sob out, "Oh, Gordy," and I bent deep inside that pine box and kissed him on his dead, cold lips. No one else need ever feel an urge to do such a thing, but for two unforgettable reasons, I have never regretted it.

As my lips touched his, it suddenly came over me that he was nowhere in that body. He had vacated the premises.

This may seem an obvious point, but to me at that time, it had not become real. Maybe the revelation was something simple, like I knew he would have punched me out if he had been in that casket. I mean, two brothers hugging is one thing, but kissing? Never. But I suspect this first revelation was more serious than that.

Until that moment, I had concentrated on the awful power of death; "Death has no respect," "Death is an enemy," "Death is not as it *should* be"—all thoughts about death. But what of eternal life? In the waxen-cold touch of his skin, I suddenly sensed his profound absence from that body. I have never again thought of him as being in the grave.

Then, as I raised up from the edge of the coffin, I heard my brother's voice. I want to be careful and accurate in telling this because it is something outside of accepted religious experience, and I fully respect the bounds of Scripture here. No one should ever attempt to hear from the dead in my view, but in this case I will argue that I did not seek the experience. The sound of my brother's voice took me by complete surprise. It came from immediately above, and just behind my head, as if he hovered over me. Here is what he whispered:

"You didn't need to be there, little brother. Between you and me there was no unfinished business."

Sweet absolution I received it, and it flowed from my head to my feet like warm, healing oil. The still small voice had not let me down after all. There had been no compelling need for me to be at the deathbed because I had obeyed the command: *Keep quiet and celebrate your brother's life.* While he still lived, Gordon and I had reached across the gulf between us, buried our past, offered our gifts to one another, and we had left nothing undone.

His words were the final piece to my puzzle. As I looked down, dry-eyed now, at the shed hull of his body in that oversized coffin, I said my final good-bye. Then I began to smile—really smile. My thoughts flashed back to the moment when I had picked up the Nikon camera feeling the anticipation; then to the ridge above the whispering Selway, when I had jumped from the saddle, running like a crazy man to get a picture I would not otherwise have taken; to the sound of the shutter as the camera recorded my finest memory of Gordon, to the voice saying, *Well done; that's the picture you are supposed to take*; to the appreciative look he gave as he rode past, to the hug at the end of the hunt, to the tear on his dusty beard and his words, "I love you, brother—" the only time I had ever heard him say it.

No unfinished business.

Today, I still grieve. I miss the phone calls, Gordon's arrogant laugh, his willpower. I miss trading manuscripts and stories, his talent, the articles and books he would have written, making a name for himself and his outfit. I miss the improvement he would have brought to my own writing, the horseback adventures, hunting and fishing we would have shared. I miss the father and the husband he was, and was still becoming. Most of all, I miss that great heart of his, that had only just begun to emerge from behind that outlaw beard. These are death's realities—the things we cannot understand.

But like Griz's story of the hand squeeze, I have a special comfort. I have the last photograph of Gordon. I share it with family, and with those friends who visit my home now located in the Rocky Mountains of Colorado. I tell them about the still small voice. I say, "I don't always hear it, but I pray that I will."

Yes, I do pray that I will.

AFTERWORD

The Last Photograph is based entirely on events from the author's life, including the last picture of his older brother. As a tribute and memorial to him, the photograph is included here.

Gordon Bransford
1947- 1981